I0550333

Dedicated to my friend and aide through every rewrite
of this novel, JIRWeeks.
To all those who have put up with my ramblings about
the Four kingdoms.
To all those that scoffed at the idea of writing a book.
To my family, old and new.
Thank you for all your support.

Still to come

*HOPES END
VESTIGES OF HOPE*

THE CITY OF HOPE

N J Hobbs

First published 2007
By N J Hobbs
©2007 N J Hobbs. All rights reserved.

(Life, Hope, Sorcery, Chaos and Saviour)

PART ONE: LIFE.

By N J Hobbs

Prologue

(December 17th 1235)

Byrad Branight rides into town his shoulder length black hair flapping in the winter wind. Slowly he guides his horse along the street, and spots a sign declaring one building to be an inn. Approaching the stable to the side of the building he dismounts and gives the reins to the stable boy.

Byrad chuckles to himself, *boy?* The Boy was probably thirteen or fourteen only six years younger than he was himself, and almost matching his own five foot eight height.

"Take care of my horse, boy." He opens his pouch and tosses a coin at the lad and turns towards the inn. He hears the boys stuttered thanks as he discovers the silver coin in his hand.

Byrad walks into the inns warm interior and removes his cloak; revealing a broad sword at his side its hilt expensive looking but well used and obviously functional. He dresses in plain leather and looks like nothing more than a traveller. He scans the crowded room and walks towards the bar set on one side next to a set of stairs, leading presumably to the guest rooms.

"Good evening sir. How can I help?" asks the stocky man behind the bar.

Byrad leans on the bar, "A mug of ale and some dinner."

"Yes sir. We have a local brew that you may like, and dinner is nearly ready: spitted boar, potatoes and fresh vegetables." Byrad nods and watches the man walk to a barrel and draw ale, setting it before Byrad he disappears into the kitchen.

Byrad waits at the bar and takes a sip from his mug, the cool ale is strong and tasty, and he drinks a third before he realises what he is doing. The innkeeper returns and Byrad asks for a room.

"How long will you be staying sir?"

"Just for tonight." replies Byrad. "I have to get to Branight."

The innkeeper's eyes widen,

7

"You live there?"

Byrad laughs, "I was born there." He looks at the innkeeper and his mood changes, "Tell me, I have been away from home for a long time, but I have heard strange rumours about Branight." He leaves the question unsaid, but the innkeeper nods gravely.

"With all the travellers I get here there are always rumours. But I've heard little of Branight."

"Tell me."

The innkeeper begins to clean the top of his bar, though it is already spotless,

"All I have heard is that no travellers have come from Branight in three months, and it's not just here my patrons from the north say the city has been closed. No merchants, traders not even the patrols have been seen or heard of."

Byrad looks at the man and nods, "Thank you." He broods for a moment then he downs his ale and asks for another. The innkeeper hands it over along with a key, a number five engraved into it.

Byrad walks to a table near the fire opposite from the bar, and sits with his back to the wall. He watches the people of the common room and relaxes. His swords hilt digs into his side, and he unbuckles the belt and loops it over the back of the chair. Seeing the stable boy enter under the burden of his pack the boy staggers over and drops it next to the table. Byrad thanks the boy and tells him to sit a moment, panting the boy slumps into the chair.

"Excuse me." Byrad calls to a serving girl, "My young friend here would like a drink."

The girl turns to the boy, who looks at Byrad and at the mans nod the boy grins and asks for ale.

"Thank you sir." says the boy, Byrad nods and moves to the bar.

"Innkeeper how much is my bill so far?"

The man picks up a slate and jots down a few numbers, "It comes to twenty copper pieces: six for the ales, ten for the meal, and four for the room."

Byrad opens his pouch and drops a gold coin into the innkeeper's open hand.

"That should cover the bill." The innkeeper nods speechless, the gold coin was five times what was needed. "Could I have some bread and cheese while I wait for dinner?"

The man nods and rushes to the kitchen, returning quickly with soft bread and cheese. Byrad leans back against the bar and surveys the room, munching on the strong cheese and still warm bread. Nearby a group of rough looking men stare at him. Byrad looks away but from the corner of his eye he sees the trio stand. Obviously drunk, they stagger and head over to him.

Byrad turns and nods to them, "Good evening."

The men surround him and the noble turns so he can see them all, one has a knife in his hand.

"We've had some bad luck at the dice today. And I think you should be kind hearted enough to share a few coins."

Byrad drains his mug and looks at the men a friendly smile on his face,

"Come on lads, you know what it's like. I haven't that much on me." As Byrad speaks he sees the look in the mans eye, without another word he smashes the mug down on the hand holding the knife, the blade drops to the floor.

Byrad slams an elbow into the left hand mans face and he follows the knife. Stepping back from the other two he watches, when one steps forward he meets him with a punch to the face, this one crumples too. Then the last falls at the noble mans feet and Byrad sees the innkeeper with a club in hand.

"Thank you." says Byrad.

"I am sorry sir, these lads have been here all day, and they don't know when to stop dicing." The innkeeper motions to some other patrons, locals, who drag the groaning men outside. Then the innkeeper hands Byrad another ale and a plate laden with slabs of meat, potatoes and vegetables.

The noble man sits and the boy stares at him in awe.

"How did you do that sir?"

Byrad smiles, "I have spent the last three years in the kingdom of Grovia, as part of the border patrol. I learnt a few things that help me in a fight."

The boy's eyes go to the sword, "Is that were you got your blade?"

Byrad shakes his head washing down his meal with some ale.

"No my father gave me this before I left; it was his when he joined the patrol."

9

The boy is about to speak when the door opens and an angry shout is heard, "Stable boy!" the lad nods to Byrad and runs for the door, apologising to the man that had been waiting for him.

Byrad sits quietly after his huge dinner, the room is still crowded and he listens to the gossip.

"... did you hear? The monks were thrown out of Gorst, they were teaching in the Staff Quarter..."

"...a group of cultists are travelling about, they are a strange looking bunch."

"...Branight is a place of evil, no one comes or goes from there any more..."

Byrad leans forward at the last and listens intently to the conversation, what he hears chills him and he falls to brooding.

The rumours were just that, gossip it probably wasn't true. Byrad sits a moment longer then stands, he nods to the innkeeper and heads for his room. Once in the small room he strips off his clothes and washes in the bowl, set aside for that purpose. Then he dries himself and climbs into bed.

Byrad tosses and turns, until he finely shoves his thoughts aside and rolls over into a deep slumber.

The next morning, just after dawn Byrad rides out of the town. Trading it was called, a self governed town not part of any Kingdom. He rides northwards heading for Agronomy, a farming city of the Kingdom of Mercia, the last community before his home city.

As he rides north he ponders the rumours he had heard, and as the four long days pass he becomes more and more concerned. His concern does not leave him when he reaches Agronomy, the town was silent and the doors and windows were shut to the night. Riding to the inn he looks at the three men stood at the door way, men armed with sharpened staffs and bejewelled with holy symbols.

Byrad dismounts and walks up to them.

"I would like a room." Byrad states.

The men look at him intently and then they move aside. Byrad sees himself in the mirror hung before him, looking at the men they nod in greeting and one opens the door.

When Byrad steps into the common room he sees at least four men stood around the door, cross bows in hand, aimed at him. His hand drops to his sword but the men lift the weapons and take their seats again. The innkeeper hurries over and offers Byrad hospitality and wine.

"Innkeep, your hospitality would be more pleasant if you removed the henchmen. I'll have ale and a room, *if* that's acceptable."

The man nods and hurries off while Byrad walks to the bar leaning on it beside other travellers.

"Not the friendliest of welcomes, is it?" says the man on his left, the one on the right has his head on the bar, snoring.

Byrad glances at the man, dressed in black leather he stands a half foot taller than himself.

"Hmm" mummers Byrad, "What's the problem?"

The man sips his ale as the innkeeper delivers Byrads mug.

"There have been deaths here for the last six weeks, the towns folk are wary now and trust none but themselves."

Byrad frowns, he had heard something of this before. "Are there any ideas as to the culprit?"

The man nods.

"They say it is the Lord of Branight, he..."

The mans words choke off as Byrad grabs him by his throat and slams him to the floor, levelling his sword with the mans face.

The mans eyes stare into Byrads, then flicker to the sword and back again.

"I meant nothing just rumours." gasps the man.

Byrad takes a breath and glances at the others around him, seeing the bowmen back on their feet again, weapons raised, he releases the man and helps him up while sheathing his sword.

"Sorry." Byrad mutters and offers the man ale.

The man accepts and after a moment Byrad walks to an empty table, sitting with his back to the wall.

As Byrad waits for the innkeeper to bring him food the man leaves. He adjusts his cloak and nods to Byrad. Byrad nods back his eyes noticing the mans odd sword and dagger at his left hip; they were both thin bladed like a rapier, but the hilt was that of a normal sword, a simple 'T' shape.

Byrad turns his attention to his food then as sleep begins to become insistent, he leaves the almost silent common room and goes to his bed.

The next morning Byrad leaves and rides for his home. He rides hard and fast, barely stopping during the five days. Racing north rumours and his own inner fears spur him on.
He rides on and on at one point he races past an inn at the side of the road, shouting apologies as he nearly runs a man over, who is stumbling out of the door.
Byrad reaches the last hill to his home, his eyes stare out over the valley of Branight not dropping once. He sees the road disappear to the north as it winds its way through Branight, skirting the forest to the west before passing over the Lake of Night, to the northern plains of the nomadic people.
Slowing his horse he prepares himself for the worst. His eyes trace the road back to the city, noting the frost beginning to form as the winter wind picks up. As his eyes reach the city he stares through the cloud of his breath.
"No!" the whispered word slides softly from his lips, his face pales to a ghastly white, the chill wind whipping his dark hair about his face.

Chapter One

Byrad looks around the room as he dries himself, he had been here for three months and it already felt like home.

Home

His heart begins to beat faster as he thinks of his real home, a cold sweat breaking out on his brow mentally he pushes the memories away and turns to the clothes on the bed.

Catching sight of his reflection in a mirror he pauses. He sees a young man, twenty years old with long dark hair, clean-shaven with dark brown eyes that are still shadowed with pain. The proud countenance of a lord's son. Shaking his head he pulls on his leather shirt and trousers. Buckling on his sword belt he looks at the empty scabbard, and silently berates himself. Thrusting his long knife into its sheath he heads for the front door.

The couple were stood near the horse they had given him. He smiles and walks over to the elderly man and wife, they had looked after him well, ever since he had stumbled upon their farm half mad with grief.

He kisses the woman's wrinkled cheek expressing his thanks, then shakes hands with the old farmer who suddenly embraces the young man.

"Take care, boy." says the old man in a rough voice, putting one arm around his tearful wife's shoulders.

"Thank you both." He says in return, quickly turning away as his own eyes blur. Mounting his horse Byrad turns towards the farm gates then waves as he says,

"I shall come back." Then he gallops his horse out onto the road.

The old couple walk back into their house, finding a small bag of coins and a note. The farmer reads it aloud,

For your kindness, thank you.

The old woman turns and cries into the chest of her husband, wishing they could have been blessed with a son like the young man who had just left.

Byrad slows his horse after a while and rides east heading for the main north/south road. Sitting he looks at the countryside of Mercia, one of the Four Kingdoms spread out before him. As he rides he relaxes and considers his next move. For the last month of his stay at the farm he had searched his memories, for away to save his people and his father. Finally he had come upon an idea.

When he was younger Byrads father told his son a story, a very old tale of a time when Branight was not even built. The founding father of that great city was a simple swordsman, until the emergence of a great army of monsters: Giants, Orcs, Trolls, and things even more hideous. The four Kings met in a historic gathering. Each signed a treaty of cooperation and prepared themselves and their armies to march north, and face the invaders. Dynadryd 'Two-handed', fore father of Byrad, joined the army of Gorst, a powerful military kingdom and his home city. Soon he had risen to captain a troop. The four armies joined and the battle began upon the plains; but the four kings each tried to use their armies separately, soon all are in retreat. For many years the battle raged, with strange creatures using powers that none had seen before, seemingly unharmed by sword or bow. Then Dynadryd, long thought dead, returned with a great sword and his troop each armed with similar weapons. With their help he halts the advance of the army, even destroying some of the creatures. Then the kings all decided that they should have a single leader, a Warmonger, they chose Dynadryd.

Byrad had remembered the story and now plans to find that weapon. He would start with the monastic Order of Knowledge to the south.

His father believed the sword to have been given by the Earth God Laumas-Nahtan. If it was, then the god owes us the use of that blade Byrad says silently to himself.

Suddenly his horse stops, looking up Byrad sees a group on the road surrounded by dense forest. The group, dirty and villainous looking horsemen stand before him.

"Excuse me sirs, but you block the road." says Byrad clutching his knife at his side.

One of the men grins showing blackened teeth, "Yes, we do." He says, his men laugh and pull clubs from their belts ready to attack Byrad.

The noble man draws his blade and watches as the bandits' charge.

He sways aside from one foul smelling oaf, stabbing him in the back as he over balances and falls to the ground; the mans scream of pain is silenced as his own horse tramples him.

Byrad turns and ducks another blow, but then pain explodes across the back of his head. Looking up he watches as a club, encrusted with dry blood, swings round smashing him from his horse to lie groaning on the ground.

With blood streaming from his forehead, his vision is blurred his senses reeling from the blow, he watches as the men advance on him. Laughing the men dismount and pick up the now semiconscious Byrad, as he is held the bandits beat him. A particularly vicious blow rips the noble man from his captors' grip. Looking up he blinks through the blood.

Suddenly the men look past him and grin evilly, looking round Byrad watches a man approach, a walking staff in hand. The man seems to grow dim and Byrad sees nothing as blackness takes him.

*

The bandits drop the unconscious Byrad and spread out to attack the man, they shout obscenities and explain the fate that awaits him. The man seems to ignore them and just as they are about to attack he raises his staff.

A bright glow beaming from his staff illuminates the trees and the bandits both. He keeps walking towards the men who gape, then as one they turn and mount their horses galloping away shouting in fear.

"SORCERER!" the word floats back to the man making him smile.

"They still know us." He muses as he hauls Byrad up, and back onto his horse.

*

Byrad sits up in a bed, he looks at a room nicely furnished and well lit. The spring morning sun beaming through the window. From the sounds of voices and movement outside his door he appeared to be in an inn.

Swinging out of bed Byrad stands, but nearly falls as his legs give way and his head pounds. After a moment his balance returns and he makes his way to a bowl of fresh water. Looking at him-self in a mirror set above the bowl, he sees his features are pale and drawn. A small scar at his temple, one he did not have before his encounter with the club-wielding bandits. Quickly washing, he looks around and notices his clothes on a chest at the foot of the bed, a piece of folded paper atop it. Picking it up he notices the wax seal is imprinted with a symbol : a base line with three upwards pointing tines.

Opening it he reads:

Dear Sir,

If you are a little disorientated then perhaps this will help.

I came upon you being attacked by a group of bandits, if you remember anything that happened next then I need not tell it, but suffice to say I helped you and brought you to this Inn. I am afraid I had to use your money for the room and healing, but what was left is in the chest, along with the rest of your gear. I hope you recover soon, for I must continue my journey.

I also stabled your horse with the Innkeeper.

(If I may suggest, you might want to invest in a better weapon.)

Yours sincerely,

A friend

Finishing the note Byrad sits, trying to remember the part his mysterious saviour had left out... His head throbs but he can not remember. Moving to the side of the room he opens the chest, finding a small pouch and his pack. Grabbing the pouch he dumps its contents onto the bed.

Byrad sighs in relief at the sight of his money, safe and sound but for a small number of silver coins.

Sitting back, Byrad tells himself to relax, the man helped him and obviously was no thief he wishes he could have thanked him.

Standing Byrad dresses and exits his room, taking a last look at the symbol at the bottom of the note, the same as on the wax seal. He shrugs crumpling the paper tossing it into the fire-grate as he leaves.

"Ah, Welcome to the *Roadhouse inn*." beams a middle aged man behind the bar, not too far from Byrad, "Please make yourself comfortable." He waves at a table, and then follows Byrad to it, "My name is Evad Semaj and I am the proprietor of this establishment." the innkeeper raises a hand, halting Byrad before he can speak, then turns towards the kitchen and calls out, "Nemarth, a gentleman needs some of your mothers stew!" Evad turns back to Byrad.

"Thank you, Evad, I am hungry. Tell me, if you can, where the man who brought me in is."

Evad shrugs, as he prepares to answer a young boy of no more than eight places a bowl of stew on the table, along with a crust of bread. Evad ruffles his sons dark hair and watches as he walks back to the kitchen.

"You'll need a drink with that." He says, moving back to the bar were he fills two tankards from the ale barrel. Returning to Byrad, he motions to the other chair opposite, when Byrad nods his consent he sits, placing the tankards on the table.

"There you are... "

Byrad swallows a mouthful of stew and replies to the unasked question,

"Byrad"

"Well Byrad, he visits my establishment occasionally, he travels a lot so I would think he is off on another journey." Evad takes a swallow of ale, glancing around the well-filled room he leans forward. "You know what, he once saved my son when he was attacked by a troll."

Byrad ponders a moment, then with the crust of bread wipes up the last of his stew. Taking a pull on his tankard, Byrad looks at the innkeeper.

"If you see the man again tell him thank you."

Evad nods and drains his tankard,

"Certainly *my Lord*." he grins.

17

Byrad doesn't miss the remark, as the man stands to leave he stops him,

"Evad is there any chance that you have a sword I could buy."

The man frowns in thought. Then he snaps his fingers.

"I don't have any, but I believe that man is a merchant."

Byrad thanks the innkeeper then approaches the trader. Coughing softly, Byrad says, "Pardon me sir."

The man looks up at Byrad, then answers a careful "Yes?"

"I understand you are a trader." The man nods, "well I am in need of a sword."

The middle-aged merchant suddenly bounds from his chair, "Oh yes sir, please follow me."

He leads Byrad to his room, and then when the door is shut he moves to a chest.

After removing a large canvas roll the merchant turns back to Byrad, laying it out on the bed an assortment of weapons greets Byrad's gaze.

"My name is Morciu, please examine the weapons."

Byrad nods and begins to rummage through the items.

Some time later Byrad mounts his horse, a broadsword at his side and a shield strapped to the saddle. Turning his mount he rides out of the stable and onto the road heading south. After a few hours he catches up to a caravan, speaking to the guard captain he lands a job and settles in with the rest of the hired mercenaries.

Leaving the caravan at the small farming city of Agronomy five days later, Byrad continues south.

For along time he finds his travel undisturbed, passing only farmers and a patrol of soldiers. Then another horseman approaches and blocks the road, the man turns and pulls something from his saddlebags, Byrad watches as the man, a minor noble by his dress, quaffs from a wineskin. Relaxing Byrad releases his sword hilt then raises his voice.

"My lord, may I move past." he calls out, dislike evident in his voice, he had never liked the petty lords that seemed to prevail in the south.

The man looks up and seems to see Byrad for the first time, his eyes narrow in his red face.

"Who do you think you are?" he slurs.

Byrad frowns as he moves his horse forward, "I wish to travel onwards."

The man stares at him then fumbles at his side, trying to draw his sword. Byrad pulls back his arm and smashes his fist into the mans face, the man drops from his horse without a sound. Moving on he does not giving the unconscious man another glance.

Travelling onwards Byrad notices a small shrine set back into the trees, dismounting he crosses to the statue of Laumas-Nahtan, God of the Earth and all things. The statue, as with all others of its kind, holds in its out stretched hands the symbol of his religion: a wooden circle surrounding a twelve-pointed star.

Looking at the symbol Byrad remembers all that had happened to him, all he had learned of this god, for this was the being his city worshiped. Had worshiped. This was god his father had been a High priest for.

With a sudden scream of anguish for his people, his friends, his father, Byrad draws his blade and screams to the heavens in rage. Gripping the sword in two hands he swings it down upon the holy symbol. With a flash of white the circle shears in half flinging Byrad back.

Looking up he sees the statue crack, then crumble into ruin. Picking himself up Byrad rips from around his neck a smaller version of the gods' symbol he flings it to the ground.

"What have you done?"

Byrad spins, sword at the ready as he hears the soft words. A priest dressed in brown robes, the symbol of Laumas-Nahtan around his neck, walks past him to look down upon the ruin.

Putting away his sword Byrad shrugs as he makes his way to his horse.

"I have destroyed *that*, as He destroyed my home." Byrad says over his shoulder. Hesitating, he turns around, adding, "Your *god*," he 'sneers, "was worshiped by me, my family, it was the religion of my entire city. By our *faith* I would expect some kind of protection from Him!" Byrad walks over to the priest, saying softly, "I returned home recently, do you know what I found? My city destroyed, conquered by evil, my father, a priest of your god, dead."

The priest paled at that, looking upon Byrad with pity, "My son, we mortals know not the motives of God, he needs our faith, as we need him. What happened in your home must have been caused by a lack of faith, perhaps your city had lost faith in God. As for your father, his crime against God must-."

The priests word cease as Byrads fist slams into his jaw, "You dare accuse them of loosing *faith*, my father would have been a missionary if not for his title!" In his rage Byrad reaches down and lifting the priest by his robes, raises his fist again.

"HALT, SON OF BRANIGHT!" the noble mans arm, his entire body freezes. He feels a presence nearby then the priest is removed from his hand, to be replaced by a powerful man dressed in armour made from white marble. The symbol of Laumas-Nahtan on his chest.

"YOUR FATHER CHOSE TO LEAVE ME HIS ACTIONS WERE HIS OWN. IT PAINED ME TO SEE THE RUIN OF YOUR PEOPLE, BUT AN EXAMPLE MUST BE MADE."

Byrad stares at the god in shock and horror,

"You let it happen?" he asks.

Walking away the god ignores him and touches the priest his broken jaw heals, "YOU WILL UNDERSTAND ONE DAY." He calls back to Byrad.

Byrad blinks feeling strange, he looks about him aware that he had been stood still for some time. Looking around the clearing he spots the broken shrine, at which he stares perplexed. Shrugging he walks away, mounts his horse and heads south, stopping only briefly at Trading and Edge.

*

At dusk on the fourteenth day from the Inn Byrad reaches Salaman, the last town before Southport. Deciding to stay at an inn, the young noble man rides through the gates just as they are shut for the night.

"Just made it hey lad" a voice comes from the gate, turning Byrad watches as the guard walks towards him. "Yes captain." says Byrad noticing the rank on the armour, "tell me is there a good inn?"

The guard nods, "Aye, the *Twin Moons* is the one to try. It's on the left as you reach the square." He points off along the street.

Expressing his thanks Byrad rides up the road quickly finding the inn. The sign depicts two moons, one white the other blue, hand painted letters spelling the words, "The Twin Moons."

Dismounting Byrad steps inside the inn, stopping he looks around the crowded room. A group of men sit at a table in the centre, playing a gambling game involving dice. To the left sits a large fireplace, lit to take the chill from the early spring night.

Walking to the bar Byrad orders a room for the night and a stable for his horse.

Nodding the innkeeper asks, "Will there be anything else sir, if I may, the cook is close to finishing the evening meal. Roast venison, seasoned with local herbs and served with a selection of fresh vegetables."

Mouth watering Byrad nods, "Yes please, and I'll have a mug of ale."

Finishing his meal Byrad sits back and watches as many of the customers leave for their beds.

The innkeeper walks over, "Anything else, sir?"

Byrad shakes his head, "No thank you."

As the man walks away, Byrad watches an old couple leave arm in arm, feeling a pang of loneliness he calls over the innkeeper.

"Yes sir?"

Byrad motions to a chair at his table, "Will you join me in a mug of ale?"

"Certainly my friend, but I think I may have something better." The man disappears behind the bar, returning with two tumblers and a bottle of dark liquor.

Sitting down the innkeeper pours out a measure for them both, Byrad lifts his glass and follows his hosts lead and downs the fiery liquid.

"Tell me," says Byrad after a while, refilling the glasses, "why did you name this-,"he waves his glass at the inn, "the '*Twin Moons*'?"

The two men down the strong liquor together.

"Well," Begins the man filling their glasses again. "My grand father built this place and the story of the naming has passed down among my family. It is said that on the day of opening he had still not named the inn, that night as he opened the doors he saw two moons rise above the building, one white the other blue. He took it as a sign and so named this inn after that sight, so far custom has been good, for nigh on a century." The man pauses, filling the glasses again, and then says quietly, "In my grand fathers day they said that twin moons was a sign of magic, of *sorcery*. Of course now we tend to forget that."

Byrad nods his mind wanders and he looks around the room, one man must have won at the dice as he shouts in joy, his companions groan and some leave. Byrads attention is brought back to his table by a loud snore from the barman. Byrad pours himself a drink and raises it.

"To moons, magic and stories told by innkeepers." He says softly, draining the glass he stands and swaying a little heads for his room.

The next morning Byrad awakes to a pounding in his head, and a mouth tasting like sawdust. Moving to the bowl of water and immersing his head, he dresses picking up his pack as he leaves.

Heading down stairs he finds the innkeeper leaning on the bar.

"Morning sir." says the man.

Byrad nods then winces, the innkeeper gives him an understanding smile, then offers Byrad a mug of tea and some breakfast.

After leaving the inn Byrad travels south. On the second day in the saddle Byrad heads towards darkening storm clouds, bunching over the mountains.

Kicking his horse into a gallop the nobleman races to the south, but soon the sky darkens and the storm breaks. Byrad is soon drenched.

Riding against the howling wind and into the driving rain, the noble man does not realise he ridden into a village. It is only when his horse slows and he sees dim, rain soaked dwellings that he is aware of his surroundings. He spots a tavern close by and soon stables his horse, waking the stable boy he gives him a silver coin and bids him take care of the animal.

Byrad is literally blown into the tavern, forcing the door shut he leans against it exhausted and wet.

"A nasty day Eh?" the voice, Byrad learns, comes from an old man sat at the fireside. Byrad stumps wearily over and lays his cloak before the flames.

"Yes it is." Byrad says, "Though it seemed to come awfully fast."

The old man nods wisely, smoking a pipe, "Are ye prepared to buy a story?" he holds up his brandy glass, a glitter in his eyes.

With an amused smile Byrad walks to the bar. After taking a room he orders a hot meal, and is told it will be served in one half-hour. Returning to the table, a mug of ale and a bottle of brandy in hand, he sits.

The old man reaches for the bottle but Byrad himself pours the drink.

After a moment Byrad asks, "Where is my story?"

The man looks at the bottle then nods, "Very well." He says. "I will tell you a story, one that has been told and retold over the years, but this story is the original, the story that holds the truth." He pauses then begins his story.

*

"Nearly one hundred years ago a man came to this village, arrived in this very tavern, he stepped over to that seat there." He points to a shadowed corner.

"He was dressed in the clothes of a *sorcerer*." Byrad suppresses a smirk at this and pours the man a drink. "He stayed here for three days then the people asked him to leave, they did not want a sorcerer in their village. The very next day a creature struck killing our animals and taking the shepherd boy.

When the sorcerer heard this he came back and spoke with the parents, he then walked off into the mountains to the north, the place the creature came from.

For fifteen nights terrible sounds came from those mountains, screams and great flares of light and fire. Then it stopped and the shepherd boy was found, bleeding and half-dead at his families' farm.

He recalled nothing of his ordeal, or so he told his parents. He told me different."

The old man pauses and nods his thanks when Byrad fills his glass again, and then he resumes his story.

"The boy told me everything he could remember of the fifteen nights. He told me that a man dressed all in robes walked up the mountain and straight to the creature. With a thunderous roar the creature rose up above the man. He just stood there arms folded, then in a voice of iron he said, 'Release the boy!' The creature it seems was taken aback by this, but then it rushed forward to attack the insolent man.

According to the boy the man stood his ground and just raised his hands. With a boom the creature was flung back up the mountainside to slam into a boulder, that boulder shattered from the force of the blow.

The creature rose and struck the sorcerer, who must have used his magic to protect him-self; for though he was flung to the ground, he fought back with a blinding light that struck the eyes of the creature. Then as the sorcerer stands he casts a spell that seems to burn, for the skin of the thing begins to blister. With a howl of pain the creature lashes out with magic of its own: Fire. The sorcerer is surprised at this but his magic protects his dodging form as he leaps away. Suddenly the creature looks east at the rising sun, it turns and retreats to its cave.

The child said this happened each day, they would stop fighting at dawn and begin again at dusk. For fourteen nights this went on, then on the fifteenth day the sorcerer seemed to under-take a ritual. That night when the creature came out the sorcerer was sat within a circle of sand. He cast a spell that enveloped them both in light, then with an earth shaking explosion they were gone. The boy found his bonds were vanished, and he dragged himself home.

Byrad sits back as the man finishes the story, he asks, "What happened to the sorcerer?"

Byrads grin fades when the old man looks up, a strange look on his face, "No one has seen him since, but people believed that he is still locked in battle with the creature, that he is fighting to escape the place he had sent them both to, another plane of existence. Each time a storm forms over the mountains and breaks, it is the time they fight for freedom."

Byrad looks around and is surprised to find his dinner being served. As he eats he looks at the old man who now seems lost in his own thoughts, Byrad leaves him to them.

Leaving early he rides to the south and ponders the old mans tale, looking to the mountains he notices pale clouds building, another storm was due that night. Turning back to the road, he moves aside for a line of black robed priests travelling in the opposite direction. He watches them go not recognising their dress or holy symbol, then he turns south and rides to Southport, largest port city in the kingdoms.

Chapter Two

Byrad reaches the city of Southport two days later, riding in through the gates he nods at the guardsmen and dismounts.

Spotting a tavern he stables his horse and takes a room.

After a long unused luxury, a bath, Byrad sets off into town going to the market quarter he buys some supplies and a few apples. Inquiring about the Monastery of Knowledge and getting directions he returns to the inn.

Just as he is mounting the stairs he notices a familiar face in the crowd, turning he scans the room but seeing no one shrugs and continues to his chamber.

After stowing his pack, sword and gear, Byrad heads back out into the city aiming for the Monastery.

*

At the Monastery of Knowledge a young man walks to a shelf, and follows the books along until he finds one section. Leaning close to decipher the words on the bindings, he pulls one book out and returns to his table.

Opening the book he sees the first page gives the title as well,

'HERB LORE'

The young man pulls a book from his pack and lays it on the table; it has a rune on the front, a base line and three upwards pointing tines, the name 'Ammaris' underneath.

He opens the book and pulls a writing case from his pack, settling down to write new knowledge.

*

Byrad reaches the Monastery and steps inside, a young monk approaches,

"May I help you?" he asks in a quiet voice.

Byrad nods, "I am searching for an ancient heirloom. One that was lost to my family over a thousand years ago."

The monk nods, "What is the heirloom?"

"A sword"

"Hmm, and your name?" He asks frowning.

"Byrad Branight." As his name leaves his lips the young mans face clears, he quickly walks to a shelf of tomes, picking a selection he lays them on a desk. Byrad thanks the man and sighing picks up the top book, its cover stamped with the words,

'War history-200 pga-176 pga'

Byrad sits back with a groan, closing the last book he rubs his eyes and stares at the lettering on the tome, *'War history-25 pga-1 pga.'* Out of eight tomes he had found almost no indication of where the sword was lost. He closes his eyes for a moment, and then hears a soft cough, looking he sees the monk.

"Sir," he says, "it is past the sixth hour."

Byrad blinks in surprise, and then quickly begins picking up the books, but the monk stops him,

"I will take care of those, sir."

Thanking the man Byrad leaves. As he passes the door he stops and drops a gold coin into the donation box, the door guard stares in amazement, and stammers the normal thanks. As Byrad leaves he hears the monk begin speaking to another patron.

The young noble man quickly heads back to the inn, just as he reaches the door the sky opens and a rainstorm breaks over the city.

Moving to the last empty table Byrad orders some food, he had not eaten anything since morning and when the meal arrives he devours it in moments. As he sits back contemplating a second serving, the door swings open and a rain soaked man walks in. A quarterstaff in hand, he moves to the fire he stands close warming himself.

Walking over to the bar the man speaks briefly with the innkeeper, then after accepting a mug of ale he looks about the room. Spotting Byrads table he walks over and motions to the spare seat.

"Excuse me but could I sit?" Asks the man, his voice very deep. He pauses and quickly putting his mug on the table, he clenches his hand and bows his head as he stifles a violent sneeze.

"Sorry," he apologises, "may I join you?"

Byrad nods and motions him to sit. When the man makes himself comfortable the serving girl brings him some food.

While the man eats Byrad studies him, for it seems he recognises the face. The man is young probably the same age as Byrads twenty years, he dresses in simple homespun shirt and trousers.

He has short dark brown hair, a few white hairs at each temple and a small square-cut goatee framing his mouth, his eyes are dark brown.

His body is slight, but healthy looking, the deep voice is almost out of place. Watching the man Byrad tries to remember him, pondering he orders more ale and looks around the room. Slowly he feels his mind getting close to the answer.

Suddenly the stranger spins up from his seat and grabs at someone, a small man who grips a book in his hand.

"STOP!" he shouts, anger and some thing else twisting his face. The thief darts through the crowded room only to run into the innkeeper. He falls over and the tome drops open at the innkeepers feet.

"Cut off his hands!" the shout comes from the crowded room.

"Now," says the innkeeper, "Give it back, I'll not have thieves in my inn."

Picking up the book the thief is about to hand it to the now suddenly pale stranger, when he spots something in the book. He frowns then pales as he looks at the young man. He drops the book in horror, then finds his voice,

"He- he's a *Sorcerer!*" he hisses. As the word is uttered the sorcerer seems to weaken, he sags into his chair now at an empty table. The entire room falls silent, the calls for the thief's hands to be chopped off forgotten.

The young man looks up, "I mean you no harm." He says softly. But on looking at the innkeeper he gasps as the man picks up the book, and turns to throw it into the fire.

The sorcerer raises his hand, palm out and snaps some words with no meaning. Suddenly the innkeeper screams as he crashes to the floor, the book landing near its owner, who hurriedly picks it up.

"He's cursed me!" screams the innkeeper, "I can't move my legs."

The patrons stand and back away, staring fearfully at the young man. The thief glances at the innkeeper then at the crowd, he stands and runs out into the street.

"I am sorry, please let me leave, the spell will ware of in a moment. I mean no harm."

Suddenly a jug flies across the room, smashing against the wall behind the sorcerer.

"Come on boys, let's teach this sorcerer what we think of *his* kind!" the shout comes from a burly man near the innkeeper. The crowd pushes forward, and the sorcerer looks up. Over at the stairs he sees his table companion, sword in hand.

*

Byrad sees the sorcerers face pale even more as they spot each other. The noble man realises the other mans mistake, then the mob break up the chairs and with their clubs raised they advance again.

The sorcerer stares at the club wielding mob and prepares for death, with his magical power depleted he could do nothing, and against this mob he doubted any sorcerer would have a chance. Closing his eyes he waits, book clasped to his chest.

'THUNK'

He opens his eyes to see a shining sword held before him, a club stopped inches away. Moving around the table the noble comes up beside the sorcerer.

"Byrad Branight." He says nodding once as he shoves the club wielder away, "Now we are both going to leave. Move aside." His tone is such that many obey instantly, but a few still stand with clubs raised, one steps forward.

"That *Sorcerer,*" he sneers, "attacked Fingast," he motions to the prostrate man.

"Within a moment he will be fine." Says a weak voice from behind Byrad and as if taking a cue from the sorcerer, the innkeepers legs move again.

The man is helped to his feet, where he tries to regain his composure. "I think you two should stay here while we call the guard." Byrad feels a grip on his arm and turns to see the sorcerer shake his head emphatically.

Byrad nods in understanding, if the city were to get involved then so too would the priests and they would most likely both die, executed upon the 'Holy Flame of Sanctification'. A practice outlawed in Branight, but not in other cities. Turning back to the men Byrad stares at each in turn, most look away from the strangely accusing look he gives.

"I do not think so." With that he grabs the sorcerers pack and staff shoving them both at their owner. Then

29

they head for the door, Byrad keeps his sword tip ready, just before they reach the exit a voice sounds from ahead.

"Going some where?"

Byrad looks up and sees the captain of the guard and two lieutenants blocking the door, cursing the young noble steps back and away from them.

The guards look at the sorcerer and the captain sneers, "Your reputation is well known to us, sorcerer." He steps forward and reveals his tabard bears the symbol of the God of War.

The sorcerer pales and looks to Byrad, the noble man understands. With the Priests of war running the guards of the city the sorcerer was as good as dead; the disciples of War were the strongest advocates of finding and destroying Sorcerers.

Byrad curses again, then with a whirl he smashes shield first through the window and rolls out into the street. With far less finesse the sorcerer follows, falling rather than rolling.

Hearing the sound of the soldiers booted feet the two men turn and flee. Soon Byrad leads them to the stables and his horse. Quickly he saddles the beast and mounts pulling the sorcerer up behind him.

Kicking the horse into a gallop they race out of the city.

Approaching the gates, they see with sinking hearts that they were closed. The two hear a shout from behind,

"STOP THEM THEY'RE SORCERERS!"

The soldiers ahead pull cross bows but when the sorcerer raises his arms and causes his staff to shine, the soldiers look at each other and drop their weapons.

"OPEN THE GATES OR I SHALL CURSE YOU ALL!" shouts the sorcerer, "YOUR HANDS SHALL WITHER AND YOUR EYES WILL BE BLINDED! OPEN THE GATES!"

The guards quickly open the gate and the two men ride out into the night.

"Having a bad reputation *can* be useful," shouts the sorcerer, "sometimes!"

Chapter Three

The two men travel through the storm, the rain drenching them and the wind freezing them. Byrad leads his horse along the dark road, looking over his shoulder he sees the sorcerer struggling along, shivering in his soaked clothing. Even as he watches the sorcerer stumbles only his staff saves him, Byrad moves to his side,
"Get onto the horse." He shouts over the wind.
The sorcerer shakes his head, "No, I am fine. Leave me." The sorcerer stubbornly strides onwards, and then collapses onto the muddy road.
Byrad pushes the sorcerer on to the horse, looking around the noble searches for some shelter, seeing a cave he heads for it.
Byrad sets about making camp, someone had obviously used the cave as shelter before, and a supply of dry firewood was stored in one corner.
Sitting, he warms himself and looks down at the man he had saved,
"Sorcerer" He murmurs.

*

The priests of Laumas-Nahtan had taught a young Byrad, all things needed for a young noble and future lord.
They taught reading, writing, combat skills, arithmetic and history. A part of that history was a description of sorcerers and their arts.
"A sorcerer," the Priest said, "is a person who is terribly misguided, they practice a magic that is in violation of all things godly. Indeed the sorcerer is devoid of religion and so will be lost upon his death, not accepted into Our Lords Palace of Forgiving.
He or she will delve into these dark powers and his soul will be corrupt, this corruption will lead them down a path of thievery and deceit."

*

"If that were true then why help me?" muses Byrad for he recognises the man at last, then he frowns. The priest had also taught him that Laumas-Nahtan was a great and caring god, the only true god to worship as

31

he created all others, and that through worship the God would protect and nurture his followers.

That obviously was not true, as his own experience had shown. Perhaps the other doctrine was false also.

The sorcerer moans in his sleep, and then relaxes. Byrad waits and stares into the fire and he soon nods towards sleep.

Byrad reaches the last hill to his home, his eyes stare out over the valley of Branight not dropping once. He sees the road disappear to the north as it winds its way through Branight, skirting the forest to the west before passing over the Lake of Night, to the northern plains of the nomadic people.

Slowing his horse he prepares himself for the worst. His eyes trace the road back to the city, noting the frost beginning to form as the winter wind picks up. As his eyes reach the city he stares through the cloud of his breath.

"No!" the whispered word slides softly from his lips, his face pales to a ghastly white, the chill wind whipping his dark hair about his face.

Looking down at the city, Byrad stares unbelievingly. Not one of the rumours he had heard in the last month had prepared him for the sight before him now. His home, the city he had grown up in was gone, in its place was a shattered ruin.

The walls were crushed in places the towers were toppled and the great iron bound gates lay broken and twisted upon the ground. Just two months ago he had visited that city, walked its streets and spoke with his people. In two months of being gone his city had been devastated.

For a moment more the young man looks at the ruins, then he trots his reluctant horse down to the gates...

Byrad starts as the fire pops, the dream brings memories he does not want, his attention is thankfully diverted as the sorcerer moans and stirs in his sleep. Byrad pushes the dream and its memories away again, he begins to heat some broth.

Ammaris awakes to a coldness that wracks his body, but he claws his way to consciousness. Opening his eyes he finds himself at the back of a small cave, a fire burning nearby and Byrad sat beside it.

Sitting up the sorcerer croaks,

"Thank you."

Turning Byrad brings over a steaming cup, "No problem."

The young man accepts the broth and leans back against the wall of the cave. Byrad returns to the fire and picks up his own cup.

Ammaris takes a suspicious sip, and watches the nobleman.

"I will be on my way when the storm breaks." He says.

"Ok." Byrad says, after a moment he adds, "Who are you?"

The sorcerer looks up from his cup, putting it down he crosses his arms,

"My name is Ammaris Morcarcion, you know I am a sorcerer." He pauses waiting for a reaction, Byrad just nods, "you don't care I am a sorcerer?"

Byrad shakes his head, "I have been taught of you and yours by the priests, the same as every one else, and have seen the executions." At this Ammaris pales, "But what I witnessed in that tavern, well it was ugly, I am sure the priests did not intend that."

Ammaris frowns, "I'm sure they didn't." He mutters.

Byrad continues, "Besides I prefer to make my own observations of people, and so far you have done nothing wrong. Though why you cast that spell on the innkeeper I do not know."

The young sorcerer suddenly looks about frantically, spotting his pack he opens it and retrieves his book.

"This," he says, "is my lively hood, it holds everything I have learned over the years. It is the most important possession I own, without it I would have no way of studying my magic. When that man was about to throw it into the fire, well, I reacted on reflex or instinct."

Byrad nods, "I suppose a priest would feel the same about his holy book."

Ammaris begins to laugh, "I wouldn't let a priest hear you say that!"

Byrad nods, then looks at the sorcerer,

"Ammaris, I will not pretend to understand your people or your profession, but I have a request."

The sorcerers laughter dies and he answers carefully,

"Yes?"

"Will you tell me the true history behind all of this, behind your profession and why we are taught to hate you?"

The sorcerer looks surprised but taking a breath he nods and begins his story.

*

"Long ago a man found a magic he called Sorcery, his name was Karmarthen, called the first sorcerer by us. His magic was powerful with it he battled a dark evil, he fought beside the human army of the Four Kingdoms. The battle raged but Karmarthen banished the evil and brought the beginnings of peace to these lands. But at a great price, his life!

For many years the art of sorcery was little known, but slowly it became more wide spread and was soon fully established.

Thus reigned Sorcery, but for only one hundred. At that time a young sorcerer was undertaking a ceremony, one which was supposed to summon a spirit to aid him in his magic. But his summoning went awry and he allowed a portion of the evil once banished to come to earth. It took over the body of the sorcerer and began slaughtering other sorcerers, over fifteen hundred were slain. Then the rest of the people of the Kingdoms were attacked.

The Kings brought forth their armies to try and stop the sorcerer, for that was all they new of the being, and with the sorcerers suddenly gone into hiding there was none to speak up for us.

The sorcerers, you see were devising a spell to sunder the possession. It was a similar spell to the one cast by Karmarthen over 650 years before, but much of the science of sorcery was lost at his death and the spell was not the same. It drained the life of almost all sorcerers, but it did destroy the possession.

Out of the thousands of sorcerers only a few hundred survived. For the next four centuries the remaining sorcerers were reviled and blamed for the devastation. And in the year 1175 my people were hunted down by many of the remaining lords, and their countrymen. Some just exiled the sorcerers but a great many other lords, the majority, were set on destroying sorcerers and so began the executions.

34

That time we call the 'Six decades of persecution.' And it is still being carried out now. Of course you know it is the religions that press for stoning, acid baths, or fire sanctification. We retreated to our last safe haven and a community is thriving there now."

Byrad nods as the sorcerer finishes, he sits back a thoughtful preoccupied look on his face. After a moment Byrad looks up.
"You all know the reception you will receive from us when you are discovered?" He asks, Ammaris nods, "Then why travel the lands?"
The young sorcerer thinks a moment then points to his clothes,
"I, we, as sorcerers should wear robes that give our standing as sorcerers, but we can not. It is by necessity that we hide our selves but we believe that it is a good time, the right time to come out from hiding. You must see the shift of peoples faith, where once it was unshaken now people are almost bored with the very concept of faith, a shift that will aid me and mine."
Byrad sits quietly thinking of his own loss of faith. Though his circumstance was unique he had seen the 'shift' himself, not least during his recent travelling, before he went home... Byrad shivers as he remembers. Looking up he sees Ammaris watching him.
"I will think on what you have said, and you must rest you are still weak."
Ammaris lies down and pulls his blanket over his shoulder.
"Ammaris" Byrad says.
"Hmm"
"Thank you for helping me on the road."
Sitting up Ammaris looks quizzically at the nobleman, "You saved me from bandits on the road north of here."
Ammaris' jaw drops, "I am sorry I did not recognise you. The last time I saw you, you had blood covering your face."
Byrad smiles as he self-consciously scratches the scar left by the bandits,
"Do not worry about it, you saved me and I thank you for it." He holds out his hand.

The sorcerer looks down at it, and then he shakes it heartily.

The next day, near evening the two men walk into the village just north of the city. Heading to the inn they step inside and move to the bar, the innkeeper peers at Byrad,
"Ah! Sir, you return to us." He beams, "Please sit and I shall bring you and your friend a meal."
"Thank you." Byrad says, turning he sees Ammaris easing himself into a chair near the fire, a look of pain on his face. "Are you alright?"
"I'm not used to riding." Replies the sorcerer simply.
"I've ordered some food, do you want a drink?" asks Byrad taking off his cloak.
"Ale I think."
Ammaris sits back as his new friend walks back to the bar, he looks about the room and when an old man raises his brandy glass he nods. Ammaris relaxes in the chair as Byrad places the ale before him,
"Thank you." says the sorcerer taking a swallow of the brew.
"Ammaris, I have thought about what you said in regard to your profession, and I think that you are right to come out, but what of the religions. Surely they shall oppose you, try and stop you from influencing the people."
Taking a swallow of ale and nodding Ammaris agrees,
"Your right, but if we do it right then we can work our way into the peoples hearts. We will just have to see."
The two friends stop talking as their food arrives, changing the subject as they begin eating.
Sitting quietly by the fire the two friends talk about their various experiences. Ammaris picks up his tankard and noting its depleted nature wanders over to the bar. Returning to the table with two frothing ales a scream sounds from outside, followed by a crash. The innkeeper moves to the window and peers out, he gasps and cowers back against the wall.
"What is it?" asks Byrad, the man just stares in shock. Looking out the window Byrad gasps as well, Ammaris joins him and looking outside sees the towering form of a giant.

As they watch, the colossus swings its tree like club smashing it down upon a group of running guards. The beast laughs the sound booming around the town.
Byrad moves to his pack and pulls free his sword and shield,
"Amm, you stay here." says Byrad moving to the door.
The young sorcerer quickly steps to his friends side, "Don't be a fool, Byrad! You'll die if you go against that thing!"
Pulling free his arm Byrad opens the door, a gust of wind and rain blowing in.
"I can't just watch as it destroys this village and its people!" With that he steps out into the storm almost instantly he is soaked to the skin, but he moves towards the colossus.

Ammaris watches as Byrad runs forward, the giant swings its club and a shower of mud blocks the sorcerers view, then he sees Byrad roll to his feet near the giant. Swinging his sword he strikes the six meter tall giants leg, but the blade bounces from its thick hide. Suddenly the giant reaches down and grabs Byrads shield arm, with a horrifying crunch of bone the creature flings Byrad away.
Ammaris steps forward and raises his hand, saying the words to the spell.
As he finishes the spell he curses as it fails running back into the room he grabs his book from his pack, opening it he finds the spell and sitting down he begins again. Saying each word with the correct inflection and sound, knowing that this was his last chance for when this was finished he would not have magic enough to try again.
Byrad painfully picks him-self up, looking down at his broken and useless left arm, the shield lying nearby, twisted and broken in turn.
Reaching down for his sword he nearly blacks out, grimly he stays awake and makes his way back to the inn.

Ammaris finishes his spell ceremony, and casts the magic at the giant, now with greater confidence, but he knows that with his magic nearly gone he is defenceless. He watches the giant turn and notice him.

In horror he waits as it takes a step forward but the giant teeters and then topples over.

Ammaris breaths again and getting to his feet he sees Byrad stagger forward swinging his sword. It buries itself in the giants neck but snaps as it hits bone, but as Byrad sags weakly the giants life blood gushes from the wound.

Ammaris rushes to Byrads side, helping him to the inn he lays his friend by the fire, turning he shouts at the innkeeper, "Get your priest, damn you!" The man scrambles from the room.

Hearing movement behind him, Ammaris turns to see a man dressed in a soaked brown habit and the innkeeper walking towards him, others from the inn crowd close behind.

The priest steps forward and Ammaris moves aside, the middle aged man lays one hand on Byrad, gripping his holy symbol with the other he prays to the Storm god Tempest.

Byrad feels the pain fade as the healing power of the priests' god envelops him.

The priest helps Byrad to his feet, "I have healed your wound, but you should come to the church and rest."

Ammaris picks up the two packs and his staff, the priest nods stiffly and Byrad takes his own. He walks with Byrad to the door, just as the crowd begin to clap the two heroes the priest stops and turns, "Thank you," he says to Ammaris coldly and the clapping stutters into silence, "But you may leave now."

"What!"

Ammaris smiles wryly as the priest puts his hand on Byrad's arm,

"Do not exert your self, the Sorcerer will be leaving this village. Now." The last is said directly to Ammaris.

"Remember what I told you Byrad, this priest is no different. Go get yourself rested if you wish we will meet on the north road." He begins to walk past the crowd.

Just as he steps forward the sorcerer feels a hand on his arm, turning a look of resignation on his face, he sees the crowd looking at him. The innkeeper holding his arm shakes his head.

"Wait." says the man, "Don't go." He sees the look on Ammaris' face and quickly ads, "You do not need to

leave, I saw as we all did that you stopped that creature with your magic." He turns to look at the priest, "where as this *priest* did nothing."
Ammaris' jaw drops in astonishment, the priest looks at the man and the crowd,
"Are you all mad, you want this, this *sorcerer* to stay?"
The innkeeper looks at his fellow villagers, who all nod,
"Well priest it looks like we agree."
The priest looks at the villagers and gripping his holy symbol he says,
"You have all been corrupted by this worker of dark arts, he will be the death of you all!" with that he leaps forward hands grasping for Ammaris' neck. Defending himself Ammaris strikes with his staff, the pine wood crunching into the mans face. The priest drops without a sound.
"Come my friends," says the innkeeper, "Ale is free for such heroes!" the crowd cheers as the two friends are pounded on the back and led to the bar.

The next morning the two friends sit on the porch of the inn, welcoming the warmth of the early spring sun. Out in the street a group of villagers work at tying the giants' carcass to a team of draft horses. As the farmers get the horses moving Byrad turns to the sorcerer.
"So how do you feel, my friend?" he asks grinning.
Ammaris, sitting in the shadow of the porch smiles, almost painfully, "Shh!" he says, "don't shout." He sips a cup of hot tea and closes his eyes, "If the pounding in my head goes on any longer I might just die. Though that is probably too much to hope for." Opening one eye he ads, "I don't think I have ever drank so much in my life."
Byrad smiles and turns his attention to the innkeeper, who was walking onto the porch from the inn.
"Good morning my friends!" he says clapping a hand on Ammaris' shoulder, the sorcerer groans and sits up, "I shall cook you two some breakfast, fresh eggs, bacon, sausage and toast."
Byrad laughs as Ammaris brightens at the suggestion, "That sounds perfect, Garnyl." The man grins and hurries back to the kitchen.

"I am not sure I want any breakfast." says Byrad.

"It will do us good, soak up some of that ale." States Ammaris looking at his friend.

Byrad nods and Ammaris finishes his drink, and then disappears into the inn to get a refill.

Byrad looks back at the struggling horses as they pull the giants body to the wilderness. Lifting his own cup he takes a drink, then as he hears Ammaris return the priest walks out from the Church opposite, carrying all his possessions. Ammaris sits and the innkeeper joins them with their food.

The priest looks directly at Ammaris, "Young man do you not see the error of your ways, people hate you for what you are. You and your kind pervert nature, now if you give up these black arts and come to the Lord of storms to repent, your soul will be saved."

Ammaris sips his tea then without getting up he replies, "You say that people hate me, what they hate is the lies you and your gods tell. *I* depend on no one for my magic, my skills I learn and develop my self, my whole life is dedicated to the study of sorcery, to the study of the very world. I am not about to give that up, and become a slave to a being that does not even protect his worshipers. No keep your *holiness* and leave me be."

The priest sneers then with a spoken prayer he releases a lightning bolt at the sorcerer. Ammaris calmly stands, but does not move from its path, the other two scrambles for cover.

Byrad and the innkeepers sight is blinded by the bolt as it strikes Ammaris. When they can see again they see the sorcerer standing unharmed, his head bowed.

The priest gapes at the man, then when the sorcerer raises his head the priest turns and runs screaming from the village. Ammaris turns to his two friends who then gasp also, for the sorcerers eyes were glowing. Ammaris grins at the looks, "Don't worry this will go soon."

"Ammaris are you alright?" asks Byrad.

The young man nods as he sits again picking up his cup, "I had cast a spell of protection on myself this morning."

"You knew he would do that?" asks the innkeeper watching the priest run along the road.

Ammaris shrugs, "No, but it was a possibility." He then begins to eat the food on his plate.

As the two men prepare to leave, the villagers approach dragging a large sack. The innkeeper steps forward, "My friends, we found this sack on the belt of the giant, we thought you should open it."
Byrad and Ammaris move to the sack and the sorcerer pulls a knife and cuts the cloth. As the material splits a large amount of loot spills out.
A substantial number of coins, mostly silver and copper and multitude of weapons, most unusable and a few bits of dented armour. The two men take some, a saddlebag of coins the rest they leave to the villagers.
Some time later the two friends mount their horses, Ammaris having purchased one from the villagers. Byrad rides to the smithy and bids Ammaris to wait.
Looking about the village the sorcerer smiles. One of the few places he had been accepted and now he was leaving, he could not suppress a feeling of regret and vowed to return. He waves to some passing villagers who smile and wave back.
Byrad exits the shop and climbs onto his horse again, a short sword at his right hip, dagger at his left and a hand-and-a half sword strapped to his back. He looks at Ammaris, who sits smiling broadly,
"Why the smile"
The sorcerer shrugs, "I just feel great." He then looks at his companions new arsenal and asks, "No shield my friend?"
"No," replies Byrad, "Not after that giant fairly twisted my arm and shield together." He pulls free his new blade gripping it two handed, then pulling the short sword with his left hand he says, "Besides I can use it one or two handed and so allowing me to use two blades at once." Re-sheathing them the two leave the town.
At the roadway an elderly man stops them,
"How is the brandy, old man?" Asks Byrad.
"Very nice my boy." the man turns to Ammaris, "Sorcerer," he says, "I have waited for nearly one hundred years to pass this on." He hands him a small leather wrapped bundle, and then he wanders back to the inn.

As they move on Ammaris unfolds the bundle revealing a small book, ancient but well looked after, opening it he gasps.

"What is it Amm?" Asks Byrad.

Turning the pages carefully Ammaris appears speechless,

"It is the book of a sorcerer," he says finally, "his spells and knowledge all noted down. Where did that man get it?"

Byrad looks back just as the man enters the inn, "It is a long story, and I think it is one you should hear."

Chapter Four

Not far away from the village, in an old abandoned mine, a group of black robed men and women surround an altar, on which lies a young woman. Long blonde hair fans out around her head, slowly she awakens and looks fearfully at the gathering.

"What do you want?" she asks fearfully.

One of the women steps forward, then turning her back on the altar she addresses the others, "We have been summoned here, from all across the Four-kingdoms, we have gathered to do our lords bidding."

"Very well put, Gillena." A voice from the darkness makes the cultists turn, and watch as a black and silver creature strides forward. Turning to the altar it looks down at the girl, its pale face splitting into an evil grin. The young woman begins to scream, but the creature raises a finger to its thin lips and though the girl continues no sound is heard.

"Master, we have do-." The priestess freezes as the creature turns on her, fury on its face.

"Never call *me* that!" it hisses, with a back handed blow it knocks the woman to the ground, "EVER!" it adds.

The woman tries to rise, and struggles to speak through a smashed jaw. Another priestess steps forward, "The Matriarch apologises, how should we honour you?"

The creature glares at the priestess, and then it smiles mockingly, "Call me Great-one."

The cultists nod, then the priestess asks, "Great-one what do you wish from us?"

"I wish nothing from you, you have done what I needed. Now I must give this one the greatest gift ever."

The creature turns to the girl who screams in silence as it approaches.

Two hours later the young woman lies unconscious upon the altar. The cultists untie her and the priestess moves to the back of the cave.

"Great-one, what do you command?"

The creature looks down at the priestess, "Keep her, she shall not awake until I have need of her."

The priestess nods then she turns to the Matriarch, speaking to the creature she says,

"Lord, will you not help the Matriarch?"

The creature looks at the woman with smashed face then asks, "What would you have me do?" the priestess finds herself made speechless by the question.

"Would you have me stop her pain?" presses Great-one.

The creature smiles when he sees the priestess nod, it steps to the fallen priestess and with a clawed hand helps the woman stand,

"You would like the pain to stop?" it queries pleasantly, the Matriarch nods slowly, but looking into the creatures eyes she suddenly shakes her head, No!

The Great-one holds the woman, then with a snarl bites into her neck drinking the blood of the Matriarch. The priestesses turn away blood draining from their faces. With the girl they leave the mine, a sucking noise following them out.

Chapter Five

Byrad and Ammaris ride into the town of Salaman and make their way to the nearest inn. Slipping wearily from his horse Ammaris leans upon his staff and waits, while Byrad stables the animals. Looking around the sorcerer wonders how long he would be able to stay, and how long he could keep his backside free from the saddle.

Byrad returns and the two men walk into the tavern. Ammaris moves to a large cushioned chair near the fire and Byrad walks to the bar.

"Evening sir," says the man, "how may I help?"

"My friend and I have been on the road for a few days and would like rooms, baths and a meal."

"Well sir I'll have the rooms and baths prepared immediately." Turning the innkeeper calls to a pair of serving girls, as they scurry off he turns back, "The evening meal is still a couple of hours away, would you like to be called?" Byrad nods and the man asks, "Would you both like a drink?"

Byrad grins and nods, "Two ales please."

After paying for the first nights lodging and the food, Byrad returns to Ammaris.

The sorcerer looks up as Byrad approaches and he grins, "You are a life saver, my friend." The sorcerer accepts the tankard and takes a long swallow.

The two talk for a while, then the inn keeper walks over and says, "Sirs, the rooms will be ready soon would you like some more ale?"

The two friends gulp the last of the drink and in unison they hold out their tankards.

Just as the man turns away chuckling, Byrad asks, "Inn keeper, are there any monasteries near by?"

The man frowns in thought, "I am not a written man, I know the same as most others taught by the priests, it's enough to do my trade. Although I have heard of the great Monastery at Southport."

Byrad shakes his head, "Tried there. Thank you any way." The man nods and walks off.

"Why are you asking about monasteries?" asks Ammaris.

45

Byrad looks at his friend, and suddenly deciding he takes a breath.

"Well, I am looking for any book of history on an old blade that belonged to my ancestor, lost to my family for many generations. It was said to have been blessed by a god. The reason I want it is that my fath-."

Byrads decision to tell his friend falters as he sees again the face of his dead father.

Ammaris reads his friends shift of mood well and he lays a hand on Byrads arm, "Tell me when you can." He says gently.

Byrad nods his thanks, and then the innkeeper returns.

"Sir, about your question, I believe I heard some people a while back talking of a new Monastery under construction in the city of Trading, to the north."

Byrad thanks the man and lays a silver coin in his hand, more than enough for the ale. The man gapes and thanks Byrad in turn.

Byrad lifts his tankard, "To Trading!" he says.

As they drink Ammaris says quietly,

"Speaking of books, that tome I received at the village, judging by its contents, the man was using a simple spell of illusion. If that story you told me was even half true then that man was truly powerful. I..." he trails of as a serving girl comes over,

"Your baths are ready sirs." She says looking at the floor.

"Thank you." Says Ammaris smiling, as he stands he allows the girl to walk past first, she blushes but is soon called away for more ale.

*

On another plane, the god that had been worshiped by the entire city of Branight sits on his throne. In his hand he holds a book, thick and old, its cover adorned by a symbol. The god ponders the tome, if he continues with the promise he had made then he would loose some of his power. But the prophecy was playing out just as the twins had said. They were the Gods of life and death, twins from a time before they claimed god hood.

When the God of life gave up his divinity he gave to Laumas-Nahtan the powers of life. This he did only if a promise was made, that when the chaos beings were at large on the world again the book of life, the holy work written by the last worshiper of Élan Vital and the source of that power, was returned to mortals.

Élan Vitals twin had given prophecy that chaos would take Branight, and the north would see the rise of chaos. That prophecy was playing out, so Laumas-Nahtan had prepared to deliver the book to Byrad at the Monastery at Southport. Only the sorcerer had disrupted that plan. Now the God had sent to the innkeeper, a worshiper of his, the knowledge of the new Monastery in Trading. He now sent the book to that place, and began preparing his priests for the loss of some healing powers.

*

The two companions ride into Trading, all about stalls and shops hawk their wares and hundreds of people hurry between them. The two men make their way to an inn with chairs outside in the warm and bright spring sunshine, unusual after such terrible rains.

"Ale?" asks Byrad as they stable their horses, nodding Ammaris slips from his mount, handing over the reins to the stable boy. They wearily slump into the chairs and order two tankards. After six days travel sleeping in the open to conserve their money, the two felt they needed it.

Finishing their drinks the two friends pay for rooms and then head out into town, Ammaris notices an herb shop, "Byrad, I need to purchase some things shall we meet at the Monastery?"

"Why not, I'll see you later."

Ammaris walks into the shop and speaks to the middle-aged woman behind the counter. Pulling out his book he begins searching for various herbs and talks with the woman about their uses.

Byrad makes his way through the town, stopping once in a while to look at the things on sale. He spots the reasonably new building still under construction. Walking to it he notices the sign, an open book with the words: *WELCOME SCHOLA,* written in all human languages, even ones not known in the four kingdoms.

Stepping in side he glances about the building, it looked nothing like the great Monastery at Southport, but only in terms of content. Sighing he steps to the shelves and begins to search the books and scrolls. A clerk looks up but soon returns to his work, dipping his quill into an ink pot and placing it to paper, copying a faded scroll.

Sometime later Byrad finishes the last book he had chosen and sits back stretching, the clerk walks over.

"No luck sir?"

Shaking his head Byrad looks at the books on the table, "No. Perhaps you can help I need to find out about a family heirloom."

"Well," says the clerk picking up the books, "If you have tried the Monastery at Southport." Byrad nods, "Then you might be out of luck. Explain the heirloom, but I probably can not help." He shrugs looking around the small Monastery.

Byrad gives the man all the information he has, and finds himself amused by the unchanged manner of the clerk. Family ties, it seemed, did not to matter to him.

The man wanders through the Monastery, muttering under his breath as his fingers skim along the shelves. Finding the book he wanted he pulls it free, turning he hands it to Byrad saying sadly, "This is the only other book that might help." Then he returns to his desk.

Byrad looks at the slim tome in his hands, the words: *The Journal of Lieutenant Mathius, year 427.* Returning to his seat Byrad begins to read the journal,

Year 427, Thaw, day 5.

It has been five days since the start of the new-year, and six years since I joined the army of the four kings. My liege King Mercia, has amassed an army of 20,000. For the last six months we have spent travelling we go to the north, soon we shall battle the monsters that invade our lands.

Byrad sighs and begins to read the entries this soldier had made. After carefully studying the book, Byrad closes the cover and rubs his face. Picking up the journal he returns it to the shelf and idly looks at the other tomes. Peering at the faded lettering on the bindings, and out of a habit formed from years studying his fathers' collection, he tidies up the shelves. As he moves the tomes into a more organised state, he sees that a large tome had fallen behind the shelf. With some annoyance he picks it up and dusting off the cover he studies the drawing on the front, a tree surrounded by a silver circle.

Opening the book reveals a page with the words, '*Holy tome of Élan Vital, life god*', written in red ink. Frowning in confusion Byrad walks to his desk, and begins to read the book of a god he had never heard of, soon he is engrossed.

*

On another plane, in an area of void, a pinprick of light appears from which a human shape forms, knelt as if in weakness.

Blinking the "man" breathes deeply then nods in satisfaction.

"You kept your promise." He murmurs and a deep voice sounds all around.

"OF COURSE"

The being concentrates and a staff appears in his hand, using it as an aid he stands and waits. Élan Vital knows that as his new follower reads and gains in faith, then so too would he grow in power and strength.

*

Byrad becomes aware of some one stood looking over his shoulder, glancing up he sees Ammaris.

"Every thing all right Byrad?"

Closing the book Byrad stands, "No. There was nothing useful, just vague hints and unsubstantiated legends."

The clerk walks over,

"Sir, I would like to lock up now."

Byrad looks at the man, "It can not be that late already."

"It is close to six hours past midday." says Ammaris.

Byrad looks shocked and picks up the book and hands it to the clerk, "I am sorry, I did not realise the time, why did you not tell me?"

The clerk looks uncomfortable, "Well, you looked so engrossed in the book I left you to it. Sorry."

"Think nothing of it. And thank you."

Byrad and Ammaris walk away when the clerk rushes up,

"Sir, excuse me!" calls the man, "But we don't keep holy books, where did you find it?"

Byrad points, "It was behind that bookcase, on the floor."

The clerk looks at the book then at the bookcase, and then shrugs.

"Here, you take it." He says holding out the book.

Byrad raises his hands, "No I could not accept it."

"Please," says the man "we have only the truth on our shelves"

Byrad takes the book thanking the man, though put off by his manner, he leaves with the tome under his arm.

Ammaris looks side long at Byrad, studying the tome his friend carries, "Byrad," asks Ammaris as they head back to the inn, "What is that book?"

The young noble man looks at his friend, "It is a tome written by the last worshiper of Élan Vital, a god that I have never heard of before."

"Hmm" Murmurs Ammaris.

The two walk on in silence, both thinking of the god.

Ammaris' thoughts however were probably different to his friends.

After what he had seen, just recently and before they had met why did he wish to bring back another god?

Hours later the two companions head into the wilds,

"What are we doing out here Amm?" asks Byrad as they step into a clearing.

The sorcerer turns to his friend and sits on an old tree stump, "Well, you could have stayed at the inn if you wanted, I may be gone for at least a day, but I need to be away from the town and any prying eyes. I need to return to my masters, the magic involved is potent and even if I were not seen, the priests of each religion would know I was there. They would hear, and I do not wish to try and escape all eleven religious churches."

Ammaris stands, adding "So I shall cast the spell out here away from those eyes and ears. You can go back if you want."

Byrad shakes his head, "No, I must tell you I find that place a little too busy, and I have always liked the out door life."

Ammaris shrugs and moves to the centre of the clearing. Byrad sits watching his friend in uncomprehending fascination.

The sorcerer makes a circle of white powder, poured from a pouch taken from his pack. Sitting in the one meter diameter area he pulls an amulet from around his neck.

Holding the trinket before him, Ammaris mummers something and as Byrad watches the amulet begins to glow the sorcerer vanishes.

Byrad blinks in surprise, walking to the circle he reaches out his hand passing it back and forth where Ammaris had been. Reaching down he touches the white powder and yelps in pain and surprise as his fingers are scolded. Sucking his injured hand Byrad walks back to his pack, pulling out his tome and some bread and cheese he begins to eat as he reads the holy tome of Élan Vital.

*

Ammaris appears in a room devoid of furnishings, a circle on the floor shimmers white.

Standing the sorcerer walks from the room going down a narrow corridor, he comes out into a large open area of the place he had studied at for ten years.

Looking around he watches the sorcerers walking about the plaza. Some of them sit, deep in study with the vibrant life of the gardens all around.

Ammaris walks across the plaza conscious of his own attire compared with that of his colleagues. While he wares his brown travelling clothes, the others are dressed in robes of the various colours of sorcerer rank. There were Students dressed in simple white, Apprentices dressed in dark green and a few dressed in the black of Adepts.

Hurrying to the right hand side of the plaza Ammaris mounts the stairs to the Students level. Quickly moving to his room he throws off his clothes, dumping his pack on the bed. Crossing to the cupboard he pulls on his own set of robes. Feeling better for the change Ammaris leaves his room, now dressed in white.

Ammaris walks past classes of students, studying under their teachers' guidance the very basic skills of a sorcerer. Reaching the end of the corridor he turns left up another set of stairs and walks along this passage to a door. Ammaris knocks and after a moment a voice floats through the heavy oak.

"Enter."

Opening the door Ammaris steps into the lavishly furnished study of his tutor.

"Good evening, sir."

The middle aged Adept looks up, showing a kind face blue eyes and brown hair, a long drooping moustache frames his mouth.

"Good evening Ammaris, how are you, well I hope?"

"Yes, master Thelmir."

The older sorcerer nods, "I would imagine you return to take your exam."

"Yes sir," Ammaris steps forward and hands his book to Thelmir, "This is all my notes, spells and gathered knowledge. I hope it will be enough to allow my advancement to Apprentice rank."

"Well from what I see here," says the man scanning the book, "I can't see any problem. But it is up to the council not me."

Ammaris nods suddenly in deep thought, Thelmir notices his pupils' preoccupation, "What is it Ammaris, are you having second thoughts about continuing with your studies?"

Ammaris looks up abruptly, "Never. I am dedicated to sorcery, and I will continue my studies..."

"But?" asks Thelmir.

"Master, I have been travelling with another for some time now, he helped me when my sorcery was discovered."

Thelmir sits back, absently he taps a staccato rhythm against the desk, "Ammaris, you must be careful, because you are a sorcerer people fear you. Though we can see a change of opinion-" The old sorcerer stops as Ammaris gasps. "What is it?"

Ammaris looks at his master with wide eyes, "Thelmir," he says in excitement, "I have important news, I don't know how I forgot." Ammaris sits down in a chair near the door leaning forward he takes a breath, "My friend and I met on the road, he was attacked and I drove the bandits away."

"Thelmir frowned, "You used sorcery."

Ammaris sits up, "Yes master, none but the bandits saw, and they could not see my face." The older man nods and Ammaris continues, "I took him to the inn of Evad Semaj, you know he is a friend to us. Then I left thinking to never see the man again, I was wrong. We met at the city of Southport, and we sat together though we did not recognise each other. I was forced to use my sorcery, for a thief had taken my book. Byrad helped me escape, we then travelled to a small village, which while we were there was attacked by a giant. We, Byrad and I, saved the village and the villagers ousted the priest of Tempest, who did nothing. They have accepted sorcery! We could go there."

Thelmir sits back, tapping again, "*You* may have been accepted, but do not be naïve. We are still a long way from being accepted by the world, remember the religions are very powerful. No we shall keep our selves hidden."

Ammaris looks down, "Yes master. Though I had planned on returning to the place, maybe make it my home."

The older sorcerer nods and makes a note, looking up he says "Hmm, if you do be careful. Oh, what was its name?"

Ammaris shrugs, "I never did find out, but it is the village between Southport and Salaman."

Thelmir nods, "Now back to this companion, is he trust worthy?"

"Yes. He has helped me and stood by me. Though he has decided to learn of an ancient god, he has accepted my sorcery."

"Good. You will know of the council's decision regarding your Apprenticeship by the end of tomorrow."

"Thank you sir" Ammaris hesitates and Thelmir looks up.

"Yes?"

Ammaris clears his throat, looking uncomfortable.

"Sir, I would request permission to continue travelling with Byrad, I have promised him my help."

Thelmir nods but he frowns.

"You ask to put off your Apprenticeship."

Ammaris nods silently.

"I will put this to the Council."

Ammaris leaves, and his master sits at the desk and picks up the book Ammaris had left, pondering Thelmir turns the pages.

Ammaris moves back down to the students' floor. Walking along to his room he picks up his pack and pulls out the book given him by the old man, his book of magic now. Leaving his room he walks to the

Library of students. Stepping into the large area Ammaris smiles and breaths in the smell of books.

Sitting at a desk with a comfortable chair he begins to read.

As he peruses the book he makes a mental note of the spells. Turning a page his eyes widen and he leans forward as he reads the spell, a spell unknown to the sorcerers now living.

Reading it Ammaris is shocked by the description, tugging his beard in thought he ponders.

The spell could be considered as evil. Ammaris studies the spell again then shaking his head he turns the page.

Some time later Ammaris walks through the gardens, heading for the kitchens. The student pauses at the centre and looks up at the statue of the first sorcerer, Karmarthen.

"We *shall* return to the world." He whispers then heads for the kitchens again.

"Ammaris!"

The young student jumps and looks around, Thelmir walks towards him.

"Master" Says Ammaris bowing, "Is there any thing wrong?"

"No, not at all, I just thought you would like to know the council have decided to meet you at the tenth hour."

Ammaris is surprised, "But master. I thought it would be at least another day."

"Yes, it normally would but they need to speak with you about your request. Don't worry, I'll let you get your dinner now."

Ammaris watches Thelmir head for his room, and then he shrugs and wanders to the kitchen.

The bells rang for the tenth time. Ammaris looks up from his book, and slips it into a new satchel, he waits nervously for his audience.

After a while the door swings open and Thelmir steps out, "Come." He says simply.

Ammaris stands and self consciously adjusting his white robe follows his master. Walking into the chamber Ammaris looks about. The chamber was eight sided and huge, great oaken beams support the roof and these are supported by massive stone pillars.

Ammaris walks forward into the open end of a 'U' shaped table. On the left and right sit the masters, three to each side and at the apex sit two others, the Grand Master and beside him on his left the Magus.

The Magus watches as Ammaris steps to the centre of the room, though his attention seems focused on the book in his hand, Ammaris' book.

The young student stops before the assembled sorcerers, with his hands clasped behind his back he waits in silence studying the Magus and the other masters. The Magus was slightly stooped though he could not be much older than Thelmir, his face is clean shaven and wrinkled his white robes with its green, black and white trim, contrasts strongly with the surrounding black robes. The Grand Master lounges in his seat, hands behind his head a complete air of apathy about him. He is younger by many years to the Magus.

"Ammaris Morcarcion," Ammaris turns his attention to the Magus. "Your teacher has told us of your request and after discussion we have decided to allow this due to your efforts at the village. You will be given four months of freedom, also you are now apprenticed to Thelmir, he will see to your learning."

The Magus glances at the lounging master who stands and taking the book he hands it to Ammaris, the Grand Master then holds out the green robes of Apprenticeship.

"Well done." He says without much feeling, and then he turns away and begins to talk to a younger sorcerer on his right who shuffles a sheaf of papers; a quill pen makes notes on the documents.

Thelmir walks over along with some of the other sorcerers, they congratulate the new Apprentice as he bows to the Magus and leaves the chamber.

The next evening Ammaris prepares for travel, putting away his new green robes he dresses in his brown shirt and trousers. Picking up his satchel he puts his two books in and slips the strap over his head, resting the bulk on his right hip. Grabbing his cloak he leaves the room.

Walking across the gardens Ammaris heads for the chamber he had arrived in. He tenses as he sees a group of sorcerer students' head his way, one grins and Ammaris knows what is to follow.

"Good evening, Ammaris." says the grinning student mocking the name.

"Good evening." Replies Ammaris smiling, his hand rests on the satchel.

The other looks at his dress,

"Going away," he asks, "hiding your self again?"

Ammaris frowns, and clenches his teeth and sighing, causing the other to grin.

"We all have to hide when we travel, you know that!" he says in annoyance.

"Of course" Says the student, but his tone and expression change the meaning to the opposite.

Though Ammaris was of higher rank, now more than ever due to his apprenticeship, Nitram had never shown him the respect he was due. The student always said things that were untrue, exaggerated, or impossible to alter and that always aggravated him. Walking away Ammaris ignores the following comments and steps into the chamber.

Chapter Six

Byrad sits near the fire carefully reading his holy book, completely engrossed he does not see the four figures creeping towards him. Suddenly a twig snaps under one booted foot, Byrad jumps and bounds to the other side of the fire, a mistake.

Cursing he draws his sword holding it two handed he strains to see the shadowy figures. One steps close and the young noble man recoils, hissing to himself in surprise,

"Ogres"

It was rare to meet or hear of any 'monsters' in the 'Kingdoms, all having been driven to the north during the time of Dynadryd, but the stories described the creatures perfectly. Vaguely human the creatures could have passed for men, if not for the over large jutting lower jaw and the sharp incisors.

Slowly the huge humanoids circle the fire, their dark armour brilliant camouflage in the shadows beyond the firelight. Two, Byrad notices carry clubs while the others have two-handed battle axes. Byrad backs away so he can see more clearly.

One of the ogres swipes at him dodging the blow he strikes back with his sword. Swinging the blade he nearly disembowels the creature, but his attack is parried by the ogres club. With a roar one of the axe wielders rushes the human swinging wildly. The swing is clumsy and unskilled, the ogres ankle gives under the strain and it collapses at Byrads feet. Grimly the nobleman slashes his blade and the creatures neck is ripped open.

The remaining ogres watch the human warily now, grunting to each other in their own language the three decide to attack together.

Byrad says a prayer to his god and readies his sword. Soon he is battling desperately, but he knows he has lost when his foot slips and he screams as a club smashes into his shoulder. A sickening sound of crunching bone echoes with the harsh laughter of the creatures. They close in and Byrad attempts to raise his sword but the pain is unbearable.

Byrad opens his eyes and waits as the ogres approach, hunger in their inhuman eyes. Then the creatures stop as they look past the defeated human. Byrad tries to turn but he falls to the ground, hearing the voice of Ammaris speaking magic. The fire-shadowed darkness is flooded with light, and shouts of fear sound as the ogres turn and run, then a crash and the unmistakable scream as one falls into the fire. Soon silence fills the clearing.

Byrad struggles to a sitting position and leans against a tree, he looks up as his friend walks over, then he slips away into darkness.

Ammaris' voice follows, "I hope you don't make a habit of this."

Byrad awakes some time later, led in the bed of his room at the inn. Turning his head he sees Ammaris reading his books. Byrad breathes deep and relaxes into the mattress.

"Awake at last!" exclaims Ammaris.

"How long has it been?"

Ammaris smiles, "Just a day. You took quite a beating to your shoulder, I paid the Earth priests to heal you. I was quite surprised when the head of the church in Trading arrived, though he did take the money. A lot of money." the last is said with a snort of contempt.

Byrad nods then glances about but relaxing as he spots his tome on a table next to his bed.

"When Élan Vital returns," he says softly, "The healing of people shall be free, all He requires is the devotion and worship of his followers. And as for those who do not worship him, healing shall still be free."

Ammaris looks up from his books, "Yours shall be the only religion to do so."

"Yes." Answers Byrad as he slips into sleep again.

*

Élan Vital stands in a void, but as his one follower falls asleep, with his faith strong and unwavering, a glittering landscape of life forms around him. He feels his power grow his back straightens and he no longer leans on his staff.

*

Passing through the shattered portal, he looks about a city shrouded in black foul smelling mist. As he advances he becomes aware of something missing, riding on he suddenly realises what it is. Not a single sign of life is about, not even a single body, as would be expected after a siege. Urging his horse on towards the palace and his home, he suddenly spots a figure up ahead.

Riding up Byrad recognises the man, his father, leaning weakly against a broken wall.

"Father?" he whispers, but the face that turns towards him is one of horrors, the lip curls back revealing the fangs of a vampire. Byrad stares in horror at the thing that had been his father, then he screams and tries to turn his mount. The nervous horse rears, just as it is about to turn the vampire rushes forward with super natural speed, ripping the throat from the animal.

Leaping away Byrad rolls to his feet and pulls free his sword, a sword given him by his father. The vampire looks at his son then his attention turns to his bloodied hand, bringing it close to his face he sniffs the blood, then darts his tongue out to lick a drop of the still warm liquid. The vampire turns back to Byrad and advances upon him.

Backing away from the Lord of Branight, Byrad watches in horror as thousands of zombies pull them selves from the houses on either side of him. Crying in sorrow and grief, Byrad turns and runs from his father and towards the gates. Zombies, appear before him but are slashed apart by his frantic swings.

Carving a path through the undead, he tries not to think of the people those zombies once were, his people, his friends his family...

*

Byrad awakens with a start the dream was too real, he could almost smell the rotting flesh of the zombies. Shuddering, he thrusts the dream away and dressing leaves his room, ordering a hot tea, not able to stomach food. Ammaris walks into the taproom and comes over to Byrad.

"Feeling better?" he asks.

"Yes thanks, I've been reading the book of life," says Byrad finishing his tea, with his attention fixed on the last dregs he does not notice Ammaris' frown, "When I return worship of Élan Vital I shall be able to call on him for healing."

59

Ammaris calls for tea and says, "Don't all priests have that power?"

Byrad nods, "Of course but my god is god of life, his power is what causes life to be, his..." his voice fades as Ammaris' face takes on a black look.

"Don't you understand yet?" the sorcerer says angrily, "The gods have nothing to do with this world or the life on it, all creation is caused through natural progression. If the gods were all powerful then why has this Élan Vital been missing for so long?"

Ammaris stands and taking his tea turns, pausing he reaches into his satchel, pulling out a huge thick tome he puts it on the table. "This is a book that might be able to help you find the sword." He says as he storms out of the inn.

Byrad watches his friend go then he looks at the tome and reads the title, *"History of the four kingdoms. Year 200 pre gods-age – 200 gods-age"* Opening the tome he begins to read.

Some time later Ammaris hears Byrad calling from the entrance to a park he had been sat in, studying his books. Looking up he sees his friend.

"Ammaris," says the noble running up, "I've found it!"

The sorcerer looks at his friend blankly.

"It says here," Byrad opens the tome and begins to read, "Year 5 ga, the warrior Dynadryd Branight travels north, most likely along the north road skirting the forest. Travelling with his hundred, for they had heard the Dark warriors they had fought were not all destroyed, and they were attacking a kingdom far to the north across the plains."

Byrad turns the pages, "Year 15 ga, Dynadryd and his men defeated the creatures but one escaped to the mountains. Dynadryd and his warriors prepared to follow when from the mountain flew a Dragon. It attacked the warriors but they struck a blow that forced it to retreat. The warriors followed it to its lair, where they found the Dark warrior and the Dragon. The dark warrior possessed the Dragon and attacked.

Dynadryd and the hundred fought the Dragon, but though they wounded it and destroyed the Dark warrior, The Hundred and Dynadryd were killed. The bodies were placed in a tomb on the mountain."

Byrad closes the book and looks expectantly at Ammaris.

The sorcerer raises his eyebrows, and waits for an explanation.

"Do you not see? This reveals the location of the Sword of Branight!" says Byrad excitely.

Ammaris frowns, "Give me that."

He reads the passages again then his face clears but he looks up in disbelief, "You can not mean... Byrad those mountains, do you realise the area that would need to be searched. Not to mention the amount of travel just to get there!"

"I know Ammaris, but I must do this. I will understand if you wish not to go."

Ammaris gets to his feet, "Don't worry my friend, I will go with you. After all how far will you get without me to save you *again?*" He says with a grin as he heads back to the inn.

Early next morning the two companions leave, beginning the long journey north. They had used the money they had gained after the fight with the giant to finance their trip. Now laden with food, gear and a packhorse they set off. They had also bought new cloths and now Ammaris is dressed in soft leather, a type of armour suggested by Byrad that works well as clothing, and a dark hooded cloak about his shoulders.

Byrad also has new leather clothing and a specially ordered cloak, it is light blue and has the symbol of Élan Vital, a tree surrounded by a silver circle embroidered on the back.

The companions travel north and re-supply at the roadside inn, that Ammaris had taken Byrad to all those months ago.

Ammaris speaks with the innkeeper and his family then they travel on.

The sorcerer turns to Byrad,

"Byrad are we going to your home?"

Byrad stares at the road ahead and stays silent, but after a moment he shakes his head and looks at his friend, "Ammaris my home is no more, it has been invaded by a creature, it has turned my people into zombies."

Ammaris gapes at his friend who continues talking, seeming glad and relieved to speak of it, "I had returned home after hearing strange reports from the north. My home was a city of undead I met my father who was one of them, he wanted me to join him. I refused and he tried to kill me. I escaped from the city by hacking a path through the zombies, before I left I saw the creature, it was vampire-like but had black and silver covering its body like armour. When I attacked, it vanished and I escaped the city, its laugh followed me along the road, I threw my sword away and ran."

Ammaris reaches over and grips his friends arm, "And you want to get the Sword of Branight so you can release your people." He says in understanding. A thought occurs to Ammaris, "Byrad could we bypass the city?"

The noble man curses, "No. The road goes through the valley, and the city was built directly on the road."

"Ok, if we can't go through the city, and can't go around it we will have to go a different way. What about skirting the forest and heading straight across the plains?"

Byrad shakes his head, "No. The forest grows right up to the Lake of Night. The city was built in the only pass to the Plains, as a defence against another army invading. I think we will have to travel through the forest." Byrad doesn't mention the horrors that 'live' in that dark woodland, he didn't need to.

The two friends reach the forest that evening, Ammaris looks at the forbidding trees,

"Tenebrous." He says the name softly, and both decide to camp and wait for the morning sun.

After preparing and eating a stew of salted meat and vegetables the duo sit and talk. Then with Ammaris taking first watch Byrad rolls out his blanket, saying a prayer to his god soon drifts off to sleep.

Ammaris sits near the fire reading his tome. He had been attempting to learn a spell from the book he had been given, it was an offensive spell and very potent. Suddenly he hears movement from the forest, looking up he watches a deer step from the trees. Seeing the human and the fire it freezes, then turns and bolts into the forest. Ammaris returns to his book and soon the night is full, he wakes Byrad and turns in himself.

The next morning the friends prepare to enter the forest. Their plan to enter in daylight proved to be unfeasible for a thick fog had fallen in the early hours of morning.
Byrad tries to light a torch put the damp conditions make it all but impossible. Ammaris casts his light spell and a glow illuminates the trees. Stepping forward they pull the reluctant horses into the forest.
After hours of forcing their way through the under growth the companions pause for rest. Ammaris is about to say something but the horses pull on their reins, terror making them tremble. Byrad draws his short sword, needing the shorter weapon in the confines of the forest. As they wait in silence they are suddenly hit by a blast of freezing foul air, then the horror forms before them.
"Wraith!" they hiss and back up, the horses froze in terror. Ammaris shouts words of magic and touches the blade of Byrads sword. The metal sparkles with magic and the noble man prepares for attack.
The wraith rushes forward and Byrad meets it, parrying the claws desperately. The creature backs away as it is hurt by the magic. Byrad follows and attacks, swinging the sword and cleaving through its misty form. The thing attacks again and Byrad dodges the strike and counter attacks cutting the wraith in half. It screams then folds in on the sparkling blue cut, returning to the spirit plane.
Byrad leans on a tree his fear and relief making him weak, then he hears a scream. Spinning sword raised, he sees Ammaris clutched in the claws of a silver and black creature.
With a fanged smile the being flings the sorcerer away, his body crunching as he hits a tree.
Byrad screams in anger as the creature laughs,
"You can not hurt me. Why not come with me, join the father you love."
"You killed my father!" screams Byrad.
"No. I offered your father immortality, he accepted. The offer is open to you also."
Byrad screams and rushes at the creature taking it by surprise, his sword is parried but the creature screams

as the magic cuts through it. Back handing Byrad the creature disappears.

The noble man picks himself up and hurries to Ammaris. He gently holds his friend and prays,

"God of life, if you are still with us, heal this man, I beg of you." A blue glow surrounds the sorcerer and Byrad feels his pulse strengthen. Getting the unconscious sorcerer onto his horse Byrad leads them out of the forest.

*

Élan Vital hears the prayer and gives of himself, his own power weakens as the prayer is answered. He watches sadly as the landscape of life fades.

*

Ammaris awakes to sunlight, warm and bright. Sitting up he sees Byrad had made a camp at the edge of the forest.

The sorcerer puts his head in his hands.

"Amm, how do you feel?" asks Byrad coming over.

"I'm ok. What happened? The last I remember you had defeated the wraith, and then I was attacked from behind." His hand goes to his shoulder, "Then I hit a tree and lost consciousness."

Byrad helps his friend up, "I thought it had killed you but I prayed and my God healed you."

Ammaris frowns but thanks his friend.

"Do not thank me thank Élan Vital."

"Mmmm" Ammaris picks up his satchel, and checks his books. Finding them safe he turns his attention to his stomach. "Have you done any breakfast?"

Byrad smiles and hands him some bread and cheese, the sorcerer devours the food quickly.

Chapter Seven

The two men are travelling across the plains when a crash of thunder blasts over head, the rain lashes them.

"We need shelter!" shouts Byrad.

Ammaris nods and peers at the land all around. As far as he could see the land was feature less, but then he spots something. Pointing he shows his friend, they spur their horses to it.

What they find is a low wall of some type of ruin, its shattered remains held no shelter for the two men.

"Ammaris!" shouts Byrad, trying to be heard over the howling wind, "There is no shelter!" suddenly his words are drowned out buy the driving rain and a crash of thunder following a great sheet of lightening.

The sorcerer hauls on the rains of his terrified mount, unable to answer. Byrad jumps from his horse and leads the animals to the low wall. Suddenly the ground is stuck by a bolt of lightening not two meters from the two men, they are flung to the ground just as it gives way. Ammaris and Byrad fall through space.

Byrad sits up with a groan, looking around he sees only blackness.

"Ammaris!" he calls, the word echoes back to him.

Then he hears his friends' voice and a point of light appears.

Byrad moves to his friend and helps him stand.

"I am alright." Says the sorcerer, lifting his hand he shines the light around. On the ground near a rock slide lie the remains of their horses. The two men quickly remove their supplies, and take another look around.

They were stood in a room they now saw twisted metal probably a stair lay near by. Ahead there was a door of oak, the only exit.

Byrad walks to the door and strains against it, Ammaris lends his weight and they wrench it open. The two look at each other then step into the tunnel beyond.

Walking forward the friends' find the tunnel to be only a short passage, they come upon another door and the sorcerer lays his hand on the handle. Without much effort the door opens easily.

"Praise the God!" says Byrad. Ammaris glances at his friend.

"What?"

Byrad puts his hand on Ammaris' arm, "I think we have been sent here by Élan Vital. This is His doing."

Ammaris shrugs his friends' hand off, and his eyes narrow in anger, "Not all things are a *divine* plan." He snaps and steps through the door.

Ammaris gasps as light begins to glow from the ceiling, he looks around in awe. He was stood in a room six meters square with bookshelves covering two walls. The third holds a huge map showing the four kingdoms and the lands north, south, east and west. A spiral stair leads down into darkness, another door and a fireplace is on the wall behind them.

Ammaris walks over to a large desk and a leather chair, sitting he looks at Byrad,

"Start a fire, I think we will need to dry out."

The noble man nods and begins laying the fire, as he works he asks, "Ammaris what is this place?"

The sorcerer shrugs as he picks up a book that lay's on the desk, he gasps as he reads the cover.

'Journal year 454, Karmarthen'

"This must be the ruins of Karmarthens tower, we are told of it during our studying. It was said to have been formed by the sorcerer himself, by the casting of powerful magic. He pulled the rock up and created his home. None ever knew were it was." Ammaris opens the book and begins to read,

"DAY ONE: The New Year brings peace to the lands, with the chaos being destroyed by my sorcery the war is ended. But the Dark warriors are hold up in the northern forest which surrounds my tower. Dynadryd and his soldiers are fighting to get to me, I know he will fail to reach me in time. A group of Dark warriors have attacked my tower, they will soon break in."

DAY TWO: The Dark warriors have beaten my magic, they search for me now. I will go to the tower top and make my stand."

Ammaris turns the page, both men were absorbed by the words of the dead sorcerer. Both recoil for the words are written in a shaky hand and the page is smeared with dry blood.

'DAY FIVE: I have defeated some of the Dark warriors, but still more are hounding me. If only I had more power! Dynadryd is near his sword strikes the warriors down, he can not hope to save me though."

Ammaris turns the page with a trembling hand, barely breathing.

'DAY SEVEN: I, Dynadryd write in the place of my friend. Karmarthen has died, his efforts saved humanity. With his magic enchanted into my sword, and those of my Hundred, we shall destroy all the Dark warriors. They have scattered now but we shall avenge this death. I go now to lay him below in the tomb he prepared. May his sacrifice be never forgotten. On my return I shall see to it that this mans life be remembered in history, I shall give the monks his work, they will keep it safe.'"

Ammaris closes the book and leans back with a sigh.

The room is silent except for the pop of a log in the fire, the two friends contemplating the last written words of Karmarthen and Dynadryd. Ammaris and Byrad echoed the friendship they shared.

"So my ancestor did have a mystical sword." Says Byrad, "Though not of a holy origin."

"Quite correct the gods had not meddled in the affairs of men, or in this world when I found sorcery."

The two men jump and turn to the voice, what they see makes them gasp. An old man with long hair floats over the stair well, slowly he comes forward. The two men back away, they could see through the him. He moves to the chair and sits, smoothing his black robes he looks over to Ammaris.

"Aren't you going to say hello to your great-great-great-grand daddy?"

Ammaris steps forward looking at the face, "Karmarthen?" he asks.

"Yes."

"But you died, I just read it."

The old man nods, **"This is what is left of me. When I died my Death spell kept my spirit here."** He stops as he sees a look of confusion on Ammaris' face.

"What is a Death spell?"

The old sorcerer looks at his descendent, "**You don't know of that?**"

Ammaris shakes his head, "A lot of your knowledge has been lost, since the great mistake."

Karmarthen frowns then his eyes narrow, "**Come here.**" He beckons to Ammaris who steps forward.

"Amm." warns Byrad, but he finds he can not move, a voice in his head says softly, *"Do not concern yourself."*

Ammaris comes to the spirit of Karmarthen, who lifts his hands to the apprentices' head. Ammaris screams as his mind is invaded, but then the pain fades and he can see within his mind all the knowledge and memories from his life. His every thought on show for the greatest sorcerer ever.

Karmarthen removes his hands and Ammaris leans on the desk.

"**Thank you Ammaris.**" Says Karmarthen, as he drifts back his gaze turns to Byrad, "**You are a priest**." The statement is tinged with scorn, and accusation. "**Do you not realise they are not what they appear to be. Why do you worship a God?**"

The last words catch Byrad off guard, and it takes a moment till he realises it was a question,

"I do not understand all there is to know about the Gods, or even my Lord Élan Vital. But I do know he is worthy of worship, he is God of Life, he is the one that caused life to be."

Karmarthen stares at Byrad and a slight mocking smile twists his lips, "**You have faith in Élan Vital, the god of life?**"

Byrad nods, but frowns when the ghost begins to laugh.

"**You fool!**" Says Karmarthen; "**You do not realise do you. The gods they are nothing of what they say, true they are beings of great power, but think: where does that power come from?**"

Silence drops over the room as Karmarthen stares at Byrad.

Ammaris looks at Karmarthen and asks,

"Magus," he begins timidly interrupting, "Can you aid me in finding the lost magic, perhaps your spell book."

Karmarthen looks away from the priest and nods, "**Yes, of course.**" The spirit moves to the book shelves and passes through them, Ammaris follows and suddenly he is aware of words that would open the secret door. Whispering the word a section of the wall opens, he steps into another room.

Suddenly Karmarthen screams in horror,

"**My Tome!**" he looks around frantically, "**It is gone, where is it?**" His wild searching of the room stops and he fades from sight, only to reappear before Ammaris, "**Apprentice, my Tome is gone, taken by the Dark leader, a creature responsible for my death, it was never destroyed. I will give you its image.**" Karmarthen touches Ammaris' temple then he begins to fades, his voice gives final instruction, "**Take my staff it is on the shelf before you, it will aid you in your quest fo-.**" The sorcerers' face suddenly grows angry, and then he is enveloped in white light and screams in agony. Ammaris steps forward but stops as Karmarthen looks up and shakes his head, "**No Apprentice, this fight was inevitable and you can not help me.**" Karmarthen turns back and looks up as he shouts in anger, "**YOU WILL NOT TAKE ME EASILY! STEALER OF SOULS OUR FIGHT IS AT HAND!**" The great sorcerer spits words of magic and the white light fades, then Karmarthen disappears as well.

Ammaris stands still, the image of the Dark leader clear in his mind, as well as his ancestor's words.

His *Ancestors* words! He never knew he was related to that great sorcerer.

Byrad steps to his friends side, "Are you alright?" he asks, "You screamed as if in pain."

The sorcerer shakes his head, as if to clear it, "I am fine. Did you hear what he said?"

"Yes." Byrad hesitates then asks, "Why did he call you 'Apprentice'?"

Ammaris glances at Byrad, "In that book you read, I assume it tells of the ancient priests of your god?"

"Yes, But-"

"Well it no doubt tells of initiates and priests and high priests. It is the same with my sorcery. We also have different ranks.

Student, Apprentice, Adept and Magus, I am an Apprentice new to that rank." Ammaris steps forward towards the shelf. Byrad reaches out a hand,

"Ammaris, What spells do you know? So we may work together in a fight."

The sorcerer stops and turns, Byrad steps back at the look of anger on his friends face, "What I know is secret, it is not for idle gossip. If ever you need to now of my spells then I shall tell you." Ammaris turns away and looks upon the shelf.

A staff of plain wood lies upon it. The quarterstaff is five-foot long, black and bound top and bottom in silver. Reaching out his hand Ammaris picks it up, instantly he feels the power of the magic within. Also on the shelf is a belt with five silver flasks, a rune indicates their use. Ammaris belts it on. Turning away he walks back into the main study, Byrad follows and the wall slides back into place.

Ammaris picks up his pack and walks to the second door, at his command it opens.

They step into another room, hooks on the wall would probably have held cloaks at one time, now they were empty. A chest in one corner is rotted, but a number of bronze weapons lay in the remains, along with a large round shield of silver.

Byrad picks it up and Ammaris says, "Take it, it is magical." The noble man nods in thanks, at both the gift and the unspoken apology.

Byrad walks to one of the three doors, one in the centre of each wall.

"STOP!" says Ammaris sharply, "We will leave by this door." he steps to the right hand door and it opens at his command. They walk out under an over cast sky, but the storm had passed. Staring up they see that they are in a small canyon of the plains, rough steps lead up.

Chapter Eight

AAAAH!

The two men freeze as the scream pierces the night. Then they head for the small rocky out cropping. The scream sounds again, but is then cut off.

Reaching the rocks the two friends peer over them, seeing two men leaning over a crumpled shape on the ground. The moon clears the clouds and they see the hideous forms.

Trolls.

The two friends also see the owner of the scream, a human female. One troll reaches down a clawed hand, but stops as Ammaris and Byrad jump out from hiding.

Ammaris raises his hands and speaks the magic, the group all wait then a small pink butterfly appears and lands on the trolls snout.

With a roar the creature rushes forward. Byrad glances at his friend raising his eye brows, then jumps down his bastard sword in hand, his shield on his arm.

Ammaris, muttering to him-self moves over to the woman.

Byrad dodges a swipe from one great club, and then blocks the claw of the other. As the talons hit the shield an audible shattering of bone is heard, the creature howls in pain. Byrad takes advantage of the creature's agony, and with a viscous swing severs the head from the creature's shoulders. The second troll roars and swings its club. This time Byrad is smashed to the ground, his own sword arm breaking.

Ammaris looks up at Byrads scream. He sees his friend at the mercy of the troll, the sorcerer shouts and the troll turns. It watches as the human raises his staff and murmurs something, then the creature is blinded by a light. Stumbling forward it then feels the blade of a sharp knife on its throat.

The sorcerer gags as green blood washes over his hand, but he moves over to Byrad pulling a flask from his belt, the sorcerer orders his friend to drink.

Byrad swallows the liquid, sweet with a faint mineral taste. His eyes widen as he slowly feels his arm heal and the pain go, leaving no more than a dull ache. He gets to his feet, Ammaris bids him rest and pulls

71

another flask from his belt, but the priest looks over to the wounded girl and stops him,
"Let me heal her."
Pressing his hands over as much of the wound as possible, Byrad prays. Slowly a glow surrounds his hands and his face beads with the sweat of exertion. Then he collapses weakly.

*

Élan Vital screams in agony, never had he felt such pain, not even when he 'died'. He drops to his knees the staff falling from nerveless fingers.
Slowly the pain fades, but the weakness of sacrifice lingers.
Suddenly he senses the presence of another, looking up he sees a black robed figure that reaches down a hand.
"It's started." Says Élan Vital as he is helped up.
"Yes brother." Says the other god softly "I will gather the others, though they have forgotten our warning I think."
The black robed god turns to leave, but stops as he feels a touch on his sleeve.
"Ackza," says Élan Vital, "how will we stop *it* this time?"
The god Ackza looks away into the dark of the realm.
The Keeper of the dead, taker of souls.
The Destroyer of life.
Lord of death and disease, the Underworld God.
These were his titles, and his powers, but his brother was right what could they do, what had once been his was gone. The god turns away and disappears.

Élan Vital: Protector of the living, deliverer of spirit.
Warden of life and the protector of the living.
Lord of life and healing, the Life God.
Élan Vital stares at the spot his brother had stood and tears roll down his face.
He could foresee the coming times, the loss of life the mortals would suffer. This was why he wept, that and the look of hopelessness and fear he saw on his brothers face.

*

Byrad awakes, soft voices talking nearby stop as he sits up. He glances about and sees they are camped against the rock formation, a small spring runs out of the rocks. He turns back as the others stand up.

Ammaris and a young woman, the one they had helped, walk over from the fire. Byrad studies the girl and he judges her to be about sixteen, maybe older, of medium height and slim. Long blond hair falls to her waist. She is dressed in black and red leather armour, a set of daggers on her belt.

The two stop and Ammaris grins, "How are you?" he asks, "This is Tammara."

Byrad realises he is staring and looks at his friend, "I am fine. What happened?"

"You collapsed after healing my wounds." says the girl squatting down, "Thank you."

Byrad shrugs and gets to his feet, "That's alright... Tammara?"

"Tammara Silvera," she replies, "formally of Southport."

"Pleased to meet you, but you should thank the God Élan Vital." He grips her hand and looks around and frowns, "Is there any food? I am starved."

Some time later they finish a meal of thin stew and bread, and sit around the fire each with their own thoughts.

Ammaris studies his spell books while Byrad studies his holy book.

Tammara lies on her back her hair fans out around her head, looking up at the stars pondering her situation.

She could not remember how she came to the plains, all she could remember is stumbling into the troll camp. Then she had screamed and was knocked down by the beasts vicious claws.

Sitting up the girl looks at her saviours, the travellers sat in comfortable silence each reading a book.

"Byrad what is that?"

Looking up Byrad looks at the girl in silence, Ammaris looks over from the corner of his eye.

"It is a Holy tome of an ancient God." Seeing her sit forward with true interest he continues "Élan Vital, Life God. This is the work of the last priest of Life. All that happened during the reign the Religion of Life is set down here. I am the first new disciple of Élan Vital, his first true believer."

73

"So you're his priest," says Tammara "the first priest of the Life Religion."

Byrad looks at the girl in surprise, and then he ponders the words.

"I suppose I could be classed as such." He looks down at the tome a new look on his face.

Ammaris looks back at his book shaking his head, and then he looks up and sees Tammara watching him.

"What is it *you* are reading?" she asks, "What god do you revere?"

"None!" he snaps, "I have no interest in the gods. I live my life as I want, not in the way another being dictates."

"Ammaris." says Byrad sharply. "She only asked. She doesn't know."

The girl looks at the angry Ammaris, "I'm sorry. What don't I know?"

Ammaris looks away then glances at Byrad for a moment before frowning.

"I am a *Sorcerer*." The inflection he places on the title is one of pride, and he sits taller, "My power comes from knowledge of this world and the forces that are available for manipulation by *my* will. Not the will of some divine power."

Tammara looks to Byrad, who nods and then she looks back at the Sorcerer.

"Why tell me this?"

Ammaris stares at the girl, "I am sick of hiding who I am. Does it bother you?"

The girl looks down at her feet and shakes her head. No.

"I have been persecuted in the past as well, though I have no love of your kind I understand what it is to be hated for choices made." She looks at the sorcerer again and smiles slightly, "*I* am a Thief."

Later that night Tammara relieves Byrad from his watch. It was the deepest black on the plains, cold and devoid of any life but themselves. The thief stands looking about, star light barely showing their camp.

She looks over at the dark form of Byrad as he rolls into his bedding, her gaze travels to the shadowed form of Ammaris.

Suddenly she doubles over her hands gripping her head, the fit passes and she looks at the sorcerer again.

"You shall not stop me this time!" she hisses walking over to him, her hand reaches for a knife at her side. As the cold hilt touches her fingers she shivers and stumbles. Looking up she looks about in confusion and backs away from Ammaris.

Sitting she pulls her blankets around her body and shivers. The sky releases a rain storm, the cold coming from more than the weather.

Chapter Nine

For what seems like hours he cuts a path towards the gates, then the zombies suddenly pull back. Turning Byrad sees his father approach, then bow in supplication. Turning once more the noble man looks upon what he assumes is the source of his fathers' condition, and the corruption of his city. The creature stands about seven feet tall, its silver and black body emanating fear.

"Son," the voice of his father comes to him, breaking through the fear, "Son, I want you to serve at my side. Come to me and you will understand the power I now have, a power you could have too!"

Turning Byrad looks at his father approach, arms out stretched. Byrad sags, then he screams to the heavens, "Curse you Laumas-Nahtan, Earth god, you who has forsaken my father, my home. I forsake you!" then the noble man turns and runs at the creature, which begins to laugh before fading away. Byrad runs out of the gates and into the night, as he runs he flings his gore-covered blade away, and wipes frantically at the zombie flesh covering his clothing...

Byrad wakes from his dream, quickly he begins packing his gear, trying to ignore the horror of his fathers fate.

The three companions break camp early, during a gap in the storm. Though it was still murky and overcast.

"No offence but we know nothing about her!" snarls Ammaris, nearly loosing control.

They had been arguing for the last hour whether the girl should go with them. Byrad had told her of his quest and she had readily agreed to come along. Ammaris had dragged Byrad aside as Tammara bathed as best she could at the tiny spring.

"Ammaris, we can't leave her here." says Byrad.

The sorcerer grinds his teeth, "Yes we can. She told us she is a thief, she has survived that life."

Byrad looks at his friend and shakes his head, "Look, she is coming with us." The priest lifts his hand, "No! That is it." Byrad walks back to camp.

Ammaris watches him go and he shakes with suppressed anger. With a growl he grips his staff with two hands and strikes a bolder.

The recipient of his anger cracks into pieces and the sorcerers fury vanishes as he discovers a magic within the staff. True he had the spell to do the same with any weapon, but this was a great discovery.

Ammaris returns to camp and they head north just as the storm begins again.

Byrad watches the rain splashing into the mud at his feet. As he slogs along his mind wanders and he finds himself thinking back on his childhood.

He had loved to roam the countryside around the city for as long as he could remember, pretending to fight monsters and save the innocent. Sometimes he and his friends would talk of travelling the lands of the Four Kingdoms. When they were grown the chance presented itself for only one of them, for Byrad had duties to see to as Lords son. It was only in recent years he had travelled, and then only to cousins in the south. His recollection turns bitter as he thinks he should have been with his father, and people when their god had abandoned them.

The new 'priest' of Élan Vital presses on determined, he prays to his God to deliver his father and his people.

Ammaris slogs through the storm as well, his new staff aiding his steps. His thoughts are focused on his magic and the words of Karmarthen. He was the great-great-great grandson of the first sorcerer, why was it never known. For his father knew nothing of their ancestry he was sure. His mind then turns to the revelation of the Branight sword, its enchantment was obviously one of the first, no *the* first Rune-blade created by the magic of sorcery. It would be a powerful weapon in any fight, even against the killer of Karmarthen.

Suddenly he remembers a dream and the feeling of hatred that was directed at him, he saw no one, but felt the presence. He shivers as he feels it again.

Tammara stares at the sorcerers back with hatred, then shivers and drops her gaze as Ammaris looks up.

Watching her feet sink into the mud as she slogs along, Tammara wonders at her suddenly frequent black outs. She still had no idea as to how she came to the plains, only that she awoke to find two men had saved her.

Then last night she had another black out, when she came back she felt a hatred for the sorcerer. The same had happened just a moment ago. The strange thing was that she felt as if she was fighting a part of herself during those times.

Shivering the young girl slogs onwards.

Suddenly the dismal weather is shattered by thunder, then, as the trio freeze a bolt of lightening strikes the ground not twenty feet away. The three friends run, behind them as if angered at missing, lightening slams into the ground barely a foot from the fleeing humans.

"This is not a natural storm!" shouts Ammaris, "It may be by the command of Tempest!"

"Why?" shouts Tammara, "We have done nothing!"

Ammaris turns his face to the girl, grinning, and shouts "I helped stop a village from worshipping him anymore!"

Tammara rolls her eyes, she looks at Byrad but his lips move in prayer.

*

Élan Vital, Life God, walks towards the meeting of deities. he had shaken off the effects caused earlier, and he walks back straight, his power returning as Byrads faith grows stronger. The god sees a pale figure in the distance it looks about in confusion. He sends a little of his power to the figure and sees him for what he is. The god pauses as his worshiper prays, the knowledge of the situation is known to him through the link. With a thought he lets Byrad know his prayer was heard and delivers information that would help.

*

Byrad gasps and drops to the mud, Ammaris turns at Tammaras shout rushing to his fallen friend. Cursing the gods under his breath he helps to carry Byrad, they struggle with the weight, the thunder and lightening getting closer all the while. Then the sorcerer spots something, across to the left of their previous course. Ammaris shouts to his companion,

"I see some shelter!" he points to a distant nomad village, just visible in the rain.

Reaching the village the three ask for shelter and the nomads welcome them. They are given seats near the fire in a large tent, easily holding the forty or more men, women and children.

The storm would not let up, lashing the tent with rain, but it seemed as if the thunder and lightening was gone.

A man walks to the companions' side, "I see your friend is hurt, I am afraid we can do little, our shaman has fallen into a sickness that will not break."

Ammaris looks across to the shrivelled form of the shaman near the fire.

"I will see if I can help your Shaman, if you will let us stay and help my friend."

The nomad nods and the sorcerer checks on Byrad, seeing the look of peace on his friends face he relaxes. His breathing was steady and pulse was strong.

Walking to the shamans side he examines the man. Finding no obvious wounds he then asks questions of those nearby, none seemed to be able to help. The shaman had been found like this that morning. His body stiff and unresponsive. Ammaris nods and begins to fall into a trance like state used for observing the aura of other things. He feels a hand on his shoulder and looks up.

"Byrad!" he exclaims, "Are you alright?"

"I am fine, and I shall deal with this." A slight edge to his friends voice makes Ammaris' eyes narrow, but he moves from his place and Byrad kneels at the shamans side.

Softly Byrad begins to pray, his voice grows stronger with each word then a soft blue glow surrounds the body of the shaman. The nomads fall silent as the spectacle takes place. For along time Byrad murmurs and the glow intensifies, his brow beads with sweat then the glow flashes and is gone.

The nomad spokesman steps forward and gasps when the shamans eyes open, those eyes focus on Byrad and his hand reaches up to grip priests.

"Shaman." says the nomad, "Are you alright?"

The shaman sits with help from Byrad and nods,

"I am well now, this man helped me. I had gone into the spirit world, as I have done so in the past, I became lost, but was found." The shaman looks to Byrad at the last.

"Found by this man?" asks the nomad.

The shaman shakes his head a smile on his face,

"No, I was found by a god, the ancient god, Élan Vital. This is his priest Byrad. It was through his faith that I have returned."

The nomads look to their shaman who then turns to Byrad and asks, "Will you teach me of Élan Vital, so I may spread his words to those of my people?"

Byrad looks around the tent, the nomads were watching the shaman now.

One, the spokesman, steps forward, "Shaman..." he begins but the man shakes his head.

"I am no longer a Shaman, I have discovered the truth of Life. I shall worship Élan Vital."

The man nods his head, "We shall listen to the teachings too."

Byrad looks around and nods, sitting he draws out the Holy book of Life and begins to read.

Ammaris moves to the entrance and slips outside. The rain had stopped and calm had settled over the plains, a watch fire had been lit and he heads to it. Coming to a pile of canvas covered wood, he sits and wraps his cloak around him thinking.

*

The Life god feels his power grow as his worshiper preaches to the nomads. He had been fortunate that the Shaman had become lost in his wanderings, and provided him with the opportunity to boost his new religion.

Élan Vital stops his travel and welcomes the growing power he now receives. He could tell his form was changing to one that was more in keeping with his high priests faith.

Then he moves off again, the area around him, his domain in the Gods Plane, begins to change. The emptiness gives way to shadowy life.

*

Ammaris ponders the words he had spoken at camp with Tammara. "*I am sick of hiding who I am.*" His words and they were true.

Since his meeting with Karmarthen, his acceptance of current sorcery life, the hiding and fear, both for the people and from the people had become too much. Now it would change.

Ammaris watches as a few men leave the tent, reluctantly replacing the guard. They speak with the guards who had not heard the words of Byrad, talking excitedly of the new faith. The men laugh sceptically but move to the tent to find out for themselves.

Ammaris stops the still joking guards and asks to buy new items. One of the men nods and they move to a smaller tent, inside Ammaris sees things of all types. Leather goods and fine materials and clothing, after a search he comes up with the items he wanted. The guard looks at him strangely but answers a question for a crafter, then accepts the money and leaves for the tent and his food.

The sorcerer walks to another tent and requests entrance.

An old voice croaks from within, "Come in."

Ammaris steps into the enclosure, tidy but packed with things that had apparently been made by the old woman sat near a small fire.

"Can I help you young man?"

Ammaris nods, "I realise it is late and I keep you from sleep, but I would like you to make something for me out of this." He hands the woman the bundle in his hand, she looks at it and peers up.

"At my age sleep is an oft forgotten luxury, or a feared necessity." She sighs, "What would you like?"

Ammaris takes a deep breath and begins to describe his needs and wants.

Some time later Ammaris returns to the wood pile and looks at the bundle of cloth in his hand. By the light of the moon briefly breaking through the cloud cover, he feels his heart beating fast in his chest.

Ammaris breaths deeply, suddenly light headed. Standing he drops his cloak and pulls on the new garment, letting its folds fall about him. Smiling to himself, strangely relieved he picks up the cloak and draws it about him. Settling next to the watch fire he sits on the wood, watching the stars appear as the clouds break-up.

In the shadows unseen by sorcerer and guards alike, Tammara watches. Seeing the clothing donned had

81

affected her deeply. Hatred had welled up from within, and darkness began to overcome her, but this time she fought it, mentally beating back the darkness and hate. She won, but it left her shivering and weak. Unsteadily she walks back into the tent.

Byrad had finished, the nomads moved away to talk with each other or to just think on the words. Byrad looks up as Tammara walks in he waves but, wrapped up in her own thoughts she misses it.
The ex-shaman walks over and begins to speak,
"You have achieved much..." the man falls silent as he comes to a loss as to what to call him.
"Byrad." prompts the ex-nobleman.
"Byrad," the man nods and continues, "You have achieved much, more than I could hope."
Byrad looks puzzled as he asks,
"What do you mean?"
"These people have known of the gods, but through my teachings, however misguided, they never looked to them as beings to worship. You have changed that now, I would be surprised if any were to turn away from Élan Vital."
Byrad smiles, "Thank you, but it is the faith that has done the work." He stands and stretches cramped mussels, "I need to get some air so I shall see you later." Suddenly a thought occurs to him, "Have you seen Ammaris, the other man?"
The new believer nods, "He left when you began speaking, does he not wish to be enveloped by the Faith?"
Byrad smiles,
"No, and I would not speak of it to him either." Seeing a look cross the face of the man Byrad frowns, "Not every one will come to worship our God, that is their choice, the faith of Life shall be open to all but we shall not force it on any one."
The man bows his head, the words he had groped for coming to mind now,
"Yes, Father."
Byrad lays a hand on the mans shoulder,
"You are the first after me, if I am Father, then you will be Brother."
Byrad turns and exits the tent.

Stepping out into the chill night air, Byrad breaths deep, his thoughts strangely calm. He had accepted his position in the new religion, and he had made it clear that the personal choice came first. He made a mental note to speak with Brother... Byrad begins to chuckle softly, he did not know his new initiates' name. His gaze falls on Ammaris and he walks over to speak, but finds his friend asleep. Leaving him to his rest Byrad wanders to the watch perimeter, nodding to the guards that catch his eye.

Chapter Ten

The next morning saw the nomads and companions awake to a clear sky. Byrad stands outside warming his hands on a leather cup of warmed goats milk. He had not seen Ammaris since last night, but Tammara was sat near by, finishing of her breakfast.
"How are you Tammara?"
The girl looks up and smiles brightly,
"I'm fine, did you want some?" she points to her plate.
Shaking his head Byrad looks around the camp,
"No, I had mine earlier with Brother Hin-lak." He had finally found out the name that morning, "Have you seen Amm?"
"Nope, *Brother* Hin-lak?" asks Tammara, "I've been hearing that mentioned a lot this morning, and I swear you were referred to as Father." She looks at her friend, "You *are* the Priest of Élan Vital." It was a statement.
Byrad nods but before he can reply Ammaris comes from around the corner of the tent.
"Amm, where have you..." Byrad trails of as he notices his friends dress a few of the nomads look at him as well. They keep clear, even these men and women, isolated as they were knew a sorcerer when they saw one, though they showed more tolerance than most "civilised" people did.
A one sided smile animates his face, "What do you think?" he asks stopping before the other two.
Byrad stares at his friend, dressed in the robes of a sorcerer, dark green, his face shadowed by a deep hood.
"Why?" asks Byrad.
Ammaris leans on his staff and looks around, people avoid his gaze and hurry about as they pack away their camp.
"Do you see?" he asks softly, "They fear me."
"And that is what you want?" asks Byrad.
"No!" says the sorcerer sharply, "All I want is respect and to go about my own business.
I have no wish for people to fear me, only to respect me and my people, to look upon us as normal men and

84

women. Our self made exile is pointless it serves only those that wish us gone." The sorcerer avoids saying who those people were, but there was no need for them to be named.

Byrad lifts his hands in a placating gesture, "Sorry Ammaris. If you wish to dress in your traditional garb then so be it." He looks to Tammara who shrugs and looks over to a group of arguing nomads.

"Right, are we ready?" asks Byrad picking up his pack, and looking about. The other two nod and they set off, leaving the new believers of Élan Vital behind.

By nightfall they reach the foothills of the mountains and quickly make camp. Gathering dead wood and scrub they make a fire as best as they can then with supplies restocked at the nomads camp, they make a hearty meal of meat and vegetables.

They sit in silence after the meal, looking out into the darkness.

Tammara shivers and asks, "Do you believe the tales of this mountain range?"

Ammaris lifts his hooded head from studying his books, "You mean the tales of Dragons, and giants and other monsters of evil?" he whispers, Tammara nods, "Don't be stupid!" he snaps returning to his study.

"Then why whisper Amm?"

The sorcerer glares at Byrad but does not answer.

They slowly drift off to sleep leaving one on guard, the night drifts by undisturbed.

The morning dawned with a deep mist obscuring the view of every thing. Noises that were heard were distorted, and their fire was seemingly inadequate to the task of warming their chilled bodies.

"We can't walk in this." says Tammara wrapping her cloak about her body.

Byrad looks at the other two and shakes his head, "But we need to search the mountains."

Ammaris, sat in his new robes looks at his friend and frowns, "Byrad, I realise you need to find the sword, but to search these mountains would take a long time. In this weather it will take even longer not to mention the dangers. Better in my opinion to wait until it clears."

Byrad stares at the sorcerer, then nods, "Very well, we wait." Sitting, with his back turned he begins to read his book.

Ammaris watches his friend and begins to apologise. Frowning angrily he keeps quiet and pulls his hood up around his head.

He turns his attention to his staff, he had already deciphered a few of the enchantments, some were still a mystery. Suddenly his attention is broken by a sound.

Looking over to Byrad he sees that the priest had not heard it, but glancing over to Tammara he saw her thief's senses had detected the sound also. Ammaris motions her over to Byrad then he quickly douses the fire, its smoke joining with the mist and picks up his pack and satchel.

The three friends stand back to back around the remains of the fire, each looking out wards with weapons drawn and held ready. Then they hear the sound of booted feet and Ammaris hisses as Orcs appear from out of the mist.

The friends stand before the large troop of bow-legged creatures. Each carries a wicked looking scimitar and shield, and are armoured in ring mail and helm. Their bodies are black and hairy, faces split into leering sharp toothed grins.

The Orcs advance on the humans, their gaze lingering on Tammara, then they attack in a rush screaming in bloodlust of two kinds.

Byrad blocks a blow on his shield and slashes through the Orcs sword arm, its blade shatters on the shield but it screams as its arm drops to the ground. Byrad brings his sword back around and slices its face.

Tammaras lithe figure darts among the Orcs, slashing and cutting with her daggers, the Orcs show only hatred now.

Ammaris also battles the creatures, using his staff with deadly efficiency. His blows drop the Orcs at a distance not giving them the chance to strike, but then one dodges the staff and swings its scimitar at the robed human. Ammaris dodges back and spits out words of magic, his staff glows briefly. The orc watches the sorcerer as he speaks, then the orc screams in agony as its right leg explodes in a spray

86

of blood. The orc collapses and writhes in pain, Ammaris stares in horror. Lifting his gaze he sees the fighting had stopped, every one was staring at the green robed man. Then the Orcs turn in fear and run back into the mist.

Ammaris stares back at the now unconscious orc at his feet, the other two come over and Byrad takes his friends arm. At Byrads touch Ammaris collapses shaking uncontrollably. Byrad leads him away and Tammara dispatches the orc.
"Ammaris," says Byrad gently, "You did what you had to. The orc would have *killed* you without a moments thought."
The sorcerer shakes his head, his face deathly pale, "I know, it was just unexpected, I had no idea the spell would do that."
"What do you mean?" asks Byrad, letting his friend talk.
"Well, I had not yet studied the spell, it was a part of the staff, an enchantment created by Karmarthen. I have never heard of any spell like it. I do not even know its name." Ammaris takes a shuddering breath and stands steady, "I'll be alright, thank you." He pulls his hood up around his head and sits on a bolder near by.

Later that morning the three friends set off on their search. With the mist burned away by the sun they could search unhindered, but they kept careful watch for any others in the mountains.
After hours of searching, back tracking and walking in circles Ammaris calls out, "Byrad can't we rest, I am tired and starving."
The priest nods and they find a suitable campsite, Byrad indicates that they will give up the search until morning.
Ammaris sinks down on a rock, massaging his back. After the fight that morning and the difficult search of the mountains, he was feeling pain in mussels he didn't know he even had, and he knew that tomorrow would be worse.
After a quick meal the trio break the mountain silence and talk.

"Ammaris." says Tammara softly, "What did you mean when you said about the name of that spell?"

The sorcerer looks up at his friends and ponders whether to tell or not.

Byrads eyebrows rise questioningly, Ammaris nods and sips his tea, "Sorcery is made up of parts, it has a beginning, middle and an end. With out one the spell will not work, but it is obviously possible to cast a spell with out *understanding* the word." Ammaris looks at the other two, who sit with puzzled expressions, "Ok, think of the first part as the Name or Description, it is the most important part, for it holds the desire of the spell. Without that no magic is possible. But if the name is unknown then the sorcerer can not know its usage, though he can cast the spell."

"So it is unwise to cast a spell that is unknown?" asks Byrad.

Ammaris smiles uncomfortably and nods, "The spell I cast was one such spell, but I could make an educated guess at its description now, and with study I will understand it fully." The sorcerer yawns widely and lays down his cup, "Can I take last watch I am shattered." The other two nod and Tammara takes first watch. Byrad and Ammaris roll out their bedding and lay down to sleep, Byrad kneels in prayer as Ammaris slips into a deep slumber.

Ammaris awakens in darkness, fear grips him as he struggles to see.

Blackness

The sorcerer tries to speak his spell but his mind cannot grasp the words. He begins to panic, then from his mind comes one word, *Mastery*. The fear fades as he 'hears' the word, then with swift words he creates a light, it glows on his palm and he relaxes. Looking up he sees Byrad look his way, a questioning expression on his face, he comes over.

"What is it?" he whispers.

Taking a deep breath, Ammaris shakes his head, "Nothing. I'll take over now."

Byrad stares at his friend a moment then nods, he moves to his bedding and is soon asleep, his breathing deep and easy.

The Apprentice moves to the fire and stokes it back to life. Sitting with it at his back he looks out at the darkness of the mountain slopes, he shivers and drops his gaze.

Opening his satchel he pulls out his spell book and runs his fingers over its front, tracing the rune burnt into the leather, following the three upward pointing tines and the base line they sat upon.

"Mastery." he murmurs, reading the rune.

Opening the tome he turns the pages and he smiles, the right side of his lips lifting slightly, he reads the page he had stopped at. It was the first spell he had learnt, the one he had just cast.

His smile broadens as he remembers the first time he had cast the spell.

*

"Students." began the teacher, "You have all studied the spell given you at the beginning of this year. You will now be aloud to cast the spell so I may judge your skill, though some of you have cast it before now." Some of the young students stare at their desks or walls, at the these accusatory words. The teacher stares at those students ensuring they knew they had been caught.

"Each of you will cast his spell, any mistakes will be noted." She turns to the first of the students, Ammaris, and motions for him to begin.

*

Ammaris starts from his reverie as a sound carries across the mountains, then it is gone. Nothing moved, Byrad slept quietly, Tammara moans softly in her sleep then rolls over and was quiet again. Ammaris returned to his book and his memories.

*

Ammaris stepped to the front of the class, and after a moment began his casting.

"*Shanatir~*" the first word of sorcery came easily, even for the first time.

"*Crona,*" the second half of the description was effortless.

"*Omins.*" as the last word slips from his lips he realises his mistake.

The Glow, that was supposed to be able to light only a meter radius, ended up ten times as large and bright, blinding those in the room.

"Ammaris!" shouted the teacher, quickly countering the magic with a spell of her own, "If you would wait after lessons, we will talk."
Ammaris walks back to his desk, listening to the snickers of his friends.

*

Ammaris closes his book and smiles to himself, the smile freezes in terror as he looks up to a pinnacle of rock lit by the dawn.
The rock was not the cause of his terror, but the bat-winged creature was.
"*DRAGON!*" screams Ammaris.
His shout rouses his companions and upon seeing the huge black-scaled creature, easily a hundred meters long, they grab their equipment and packs and run. The monstrous thing lifts off from the rock and a roar shatters the silence.
Ammaris, Byrad and Tammara race into the mountains, unknowing of their destination or direction, they just run. Dodging rocks and loose stone the trio scramble up the mountains.
Ammaris glances back once but he is thrown forward by the blow back from the Dragons fiery breath. Muttering and leaping to his feet again, he races past the other two and heads for a cave up ahead. The other two leap into the cave, just as another blast of fire bakes the rocks behind their fleeing forms.
Huddled in the cave they cringe as the beast lets out a roar of anger.

Ammaris stands quickly and peers around the cave entrance. The Dragon lands amid a jumble of rock, its great size crushing the stone and shaking the mountains.
"Dragon." says Ammaris again.
Tammara doubled up and breathing hard glances at the sorcerer, "Oh, you don't say. I am sure we would *never* have guessed!" She says sarcastically.
"Quiet, both of you." snaps Byrad looking to the rear of the cave, "Ammaris, I need a light."
Ammaris mutters words of sorcery and a glow appears on the end of his staff.
By the light of the magic they see that the end of the cave is strewn with rubble. A tunnel leading further into the mountain is half blocked, quickly Byrad and

90

Tammara begin digging. Ammaris watches the tunnel and holds his staff, lighting the cave.

Quickly the two dig away the stones filling the passage.

Ammaris seeing a shadow at the cave mouth hisses over his shoulder, "Hurry!" the other two curse him but redouble their efforts.

Ammaris gasps as an eye peers at them from the outside, then a great breath is taken. Tammara disappears and then Ammaris is grabbed by Byrad and pushed through the hole. Ammaris falls and a great blast of fire follows Byrad through the opening singeing his back.

With a grunt they land and look up as the fire melts the rock and seals the entrance, a roar of anger fills the night sky.

Byrad groans in agony his back feeling like it were on fire. Ammaris comes over gagging on the stench of burned flesh, he holds out a silver flask and Byrad drinks the liquid down.

"Now rest a moment Byrad." Ammaris looks around and Tammara walks over.

They were at the bottom of stone stairs the exit at the top was solid rock, melted by the Dragon-fire. The room was not large, about twenty meters round, a door made from wood seems the only entrance or exit. All about the floor are the bony remains of what had once been men. They all show signs of violent death, but only one lot of skeletal warriors remain.

Byrad stands though still pained by his back, he ignores it. The wound would heal as the magic took effect, the noble man become priest examines the remains.

"This is like a tomb. I wonder what killed them." He says, turning to his companions, he is about to speak when Tammara interrupts.

"Well this is great!" storms Tammara suddenly, "You rescue me from Trolls, but then you take me on a march to a place that is home to all kind of monsters. Orcs attack us and you get me chased half way through these mountains by a Dragon! And now you are worrying about the remains of the dead!"

"You did insist on coming." Points out Ammaris he steps back as she points at him, her face twisting in anger.

"And where was your *sorcery*?" she asks ignoring him, "You could do nothing could you?" she accuses, "Your magic is useless!"

Now it was Ammaris who turned angry. With a snarl he lashes out with a fist, and even though he pulls back so as to not strike she collapses to the floor.

Byrad grabs his arm with an exclamation, but Ammaris shrugs him off.

Looking down on the thief he snarls, "You question my magic! Do you wish to see sorcery?" with raised hand he begins casting, the staff glows.

"***Mutast-***" Ammaris is knocked to the ground his spell interrupted, standing he whirls on Byrad,

"You Bastard!" he screams, "What do you think you're doing!"

Byrad helps Tammara up,

"What am *I* doing?" he asks, "You should answer that your self, calm down. Tammara was upset she did not mean what she said." Tammara seems about to speak but Byrad silences her with a look.

Ammaris, breathing hard struggles to relax. He moves away and sits on the steps, pulling his hood up around his face, his knuckles are white as he grips his staff.

Byrad watches his friend a moment then walks to the door, it was still strong and locked. Tammara fishes out a number of lock picks and crosses to the door.

"Do you think you can pick it?" asks Byrad.

*

Ammaris stares at the thief as she looks at the door he feels horrified at his actions. Would he have really have cast the spell? The sorcerer shudders as he can not say he would have stopped him self. He shudders again then stands and walks over to his companions.

*

The thief smiles and shrugs her shoulders, she squints into the lock, then the light increases as Ammaris walks over. With out a word he illuminates the door, he keeps his hood up and does not look at Byrad.

Soon a sharp click is heard and Tammara opens the door with a push, surprisingly the door opens soundlessly.

The door leads into a tunnel that heads back into the mountains. Just after the doorway lie the remains of fighting men, their weapons still clasped in their dead hands, bodies protected by dented armour. As they move on they see the passage is littered with the human remains, and others of similar build, though with sharp tusks protruding from the lower jaw. The companions glance at each other, knowing the sight of Orcs.

Byrad stops and looks up and down the passage, "I wonder what happened." he says with a glance at Tammara.

Ammaris stoops and peers at the soldiers armour as he brings his light closer.

Byrad walks over, "What is it, Amm?"

Ammaris stands and stares at the remains as he answers, tugging his beard as he does so, "The men were attempting to escape the tunnel, but the Orcs attacked them, they obviously fought a running battle and made it through the door. These men held off the Orcs, but those in the room were killed by others and were stopped from escaping. It was a massacre."

Byrad bows his head and begins murmuring a prayer, he does not see the look of contempt Ammaris shoots him.

Soon they move on and leave the remains behind.

They crouch together at the entrance to a room, it is the first area that has a man made look.

Stone blocks cut and fitted tightly together, a set of stairs lead down at one side and a pair of oak doors, one on the left wall and one straight ahead, exit the room. Torches set in brackets provide light.

Ammaris taps Byrad on the arm, "Can we rest here?"

Byrad turns to his friend and opens his mouth to speak, but before he can say a word they hear the sound of booted feet on the stairs.

Quickly Tammara moves to the lip of the stairs so who ever comes up has their back to her. Byrad readies his sword and shield while Ammaris stands beside him, staff in hand. They hear orc voices talking in their own hideous tongue.

"I tell yoouz," grunts one orc, "I hear humans!"

"Aw shudup," snaps another back handing it around the head, "Yoouz was hearin' fings!"

Their companion begins to laugh, but he chokes it off as he reaches the top of the stairs and sees two humans.

"HUMANS!" it roars, dragging free its sword as its comrades rush to its side.

"ZACKASH!" roars the lead orc as it sees Byrad and Ammaris, its companions arrive quickly and draw their scimitars.

Byrad steps forward to attack the first orc, this one carries a shield also. The priest swings low, unexpectedly the orc jumps over the blade, bringing its own sword swinging down towards Byrads head. Desperately he blocks with his shield, the sword of the orc flares with magic and the two are thrown backwards.

Ammaris blocks the orcs swipe and sees the flash. Recognising it as sorcery he knocks his opponents sword flying, running to his friends side.

Tammara had been waiting at the stairs and now the last orc turns back to get reinforcements. With a scream she leaps into it, knocking it down she slashes at its face. Her blades cut deep and its scream is silenced as its throat fills with blood.

Byrad picks himself up and looks to the orc as it stands, Ammaris reaching his side.

"Was that magic?" asks Byrad.

Ammaris nods and looks at the sword in the Orcs hand, runes glimmer through the dirt and dried blood.

"I would imagine it just found the weapon."

The orc begins to laugh,

"No sorcerer I not found. I make." The orc lifts its clawed hands and begins to cast a spell. Byrad steps forward but the other orc blocks his path and he has to defend him self.

Ammaris listens to the orc and is able to decipher the spell being cast. Realising their imminent danger the apprentice begins casting himself, his staff begins to glow as he uses its spell.

The orc finishes its incantation and Byrad and his opponent gape as the creature grows in size. Soon it is close to eight feet tall, and it heads for the sorcerer.

Byrad lops the head off the orc beside him and rushes to his friends aid. Tammara leaps upon its back but is flung off and lands at the tunnel mouth.

"Mutastrimia, Tori~" As Ammaris casts the spell he becomes aware of another enchantment within the staff, and he shouts out the command for it,

"Potanastal"

Just as the giant orc throws Byrad back against the wall, Ammaris' spell finishes. With a low roar a wind explodes from Ammaris. The expenditure of magic forces Ammaris to his knees, but he watches as the giant struggles against the wind.

For a moment it holds, then it is lifted and slammed against the ceiling, walls and the floor to leave it bloodied and broken in a corner.

In the silence that follows, only the heavy breathing of Byrad and Tammara is heard.

Ammaris leans on his staff and climbs to his feet. Standing he stares at the blood-splattered walls and the ruined mass of flesh in the corner.

Tammara and Byrad move to the sorcerers' side and look at the mess before them.

Drip, drip, drip, the blood finds the steps.

Byrad takes Ammaris' arm, the young sorcerer starts at the touch but moves off with his friend.

"Ammaris are you alright?"

Ammaris looks at his friend and takes a deep breath, nodding.

"Yes, I'll be all right. It's just these spells that Karmarthen devised their so destructive, none of our spells are like them."

The priest purses his lips in thought, and then he nods to himself, "From what we have learnt from the books and everything, the time of Karmarthen and Dynadryd was unsettled and dangerous. These spells are obviously a product of those times."

Ammaris nods in understanding and clasps his friends arm, taking a breath he turns. Returning to the stairs Tammara joins them, and they move down deeper into the mountains.

The companions reach the bottom of the stairs and find them selves in another room. This one has stairs leading down and four doors set in the centre of each wall. Byrad walks to one and finds it locked, the others also find theirs locked. Then Ammaris tries the last door and it opens. Grinning he steps into the room with a bow, then with a shout of surprise he drops.

Byrad runs to the room and sees a wide hole in the floor, from its dark opening they could hear a faint scream then a splash.

Byrad kneels and shouts down the hole.

Tammara touches his shoulder and motions to the stairs, but shrugs as well, "That is obviously a well, see the holes once used as stays for the timber framework. We may find the water source but it's not likely."
Byrad nods but heads for the stairs. Tammara looks at the well and grins, then hurries to catch Byrad, shaking her head as if to clear it.

Chapter Eleven

Reaching the next floor the two companions stop it was dark. Tammara runs up stairs and returns with torches, in the flickering light they see a mass of small skeletons. They look at each other both thinking the same: children.
Byrad steps forward and begins praying over them, but stops as he notices weapons in their hands, stooping he sees the remains were not human. The bones were of a small stature but thick and heavy, the skulls were overly large, as was the chest.
He looks about and sees a lot of other remains mixed in with the rest, orc remains.
"A great battle was fought here." He says quietly, unconsciously lowering his voice in the shadowy flicker of torch flame. The room seemed unwitting to have its age-old silence broken, still Byrad bows his head and prays for their souls.

Tammara stands nearby, her face shadowed from the light and from fear. She could hear the voice inside, incessant and growing stronger. It asked for her help, giving promises of great things for her. Tammara was tempted, dared to listen to the whispers, she seemed to have no choice.
Suddenly the voice stops, she looks up and sees Byrad walk over.
"Are you ok?"
Tammara smiles and nods,
"Yes. What now?"
Byrad looks around the room and heads for the only exit, a pair of huge double doors, open and showing ancient signs of damage. A large locking beam was split in half and the doors were cracked and splintered.

*

Ammaris awakens cold, wet and shivering, crawling forward he drags himself from the underground river.
Panting in exhaustion Ammaris lays in the darkness, finally sitting up he looks about.
Blackness

Straining to see he realises he still grips his staff, breathing rapidly the fear growing he says a word,

"Rack-" a cough stops his word as his breathing sucks in dust, after a moment of harsh coughing he gasps out the word.

"Rackpuah." instantly a glow appears on his staff lighting up his immediate surroundings.

He was on a thin section of rocky shoreline running along side a fast flowing river, rock glistens wetly in the glow from the magical light. Standing the sorcerer shivers and leans on his staff, looking left then right he turns left and walks away from the river.

After some time Ammaris looks ahead and sees the tell-tale flickering of torch light on the rocks, and the sound of miners. With a word the glow is gone from his staff and he moves forward carefully.

Creeping along, Ammaris reaches a tunnel entrance. Peering round he stifles a gasp.

*

Byrad and Tammara had been searching for hours, always heading down. They had fought Orcs and trolls, even some monsters they had never heard of, but none had stopped their progress.

Now they stopped.

They were in a large cavern it was full of ancient work areas. Forges and tanneries, bakeries and breweries, jewellers and stone masons. All were different but all were abandoned.

There were remains of the things that had once been made. Half-finished statues, rusted weapons and tools, jewellery of silver, gold and bronze set with precious stones. The workmanship of these things was incredible, and even the tarnished bronze seemed beautiful.

Tammara, over Byrads wishes takes some of the jewellery dropping it into her pouch, then the duo head down another stair.

Tammara follows Byrad down the stairs and into the next tunnel, she talks.

"Who are you?" she asks silently of her secret voice.

"I am one that can bring you all." The voice echoes in her head quiet but clear.

"What can you 'bring' me?"

98

"What you desire POWER!"
"I don't..."
The voice hisses with laughter,
"Oh but you do. When you became a thief you stole from only the powerful the influential. Your secret desires forced you close to those you hated but wanted to be."
The voice stops and seems to wait, Tammara thinks back to those days. Was *it* correct, did she crave the power that she had seen produce so much pain and suffering, to her and others.
"Power, yes I've wanted power."
"Good. I can give it to you."
"How can you give me that?" Tammara asks, feeling scared but exited.
"Relax your mind let me free." Tammara feels the voice press forward, forcing her thoughts away. Suddenly she is frightened and screams.
"NOOO"

"NOOO" Byrad turns in surprise, seeing Tammara screaming, and seemingly in pain.
Byrad comes to her side and grabs her arm, "What is it?"
Tammara grips her head and screams, then she looks up at Byrad and with a snarl she hits him. The priest is launched down the tunnel and slams into a wall.
Byrad looks at his friend in shock, she drops to her knees and shakes violently then she slumps, breathing heavily.
Byrad, sword drawn cautiously approaches the thief. She looks up and stares at Byrad and he is shocked by what he sees in her gaze; fear and relief and a peculiar expression of expectation.
"Are you alright?" he asks, "What happened?"
The expression of expectation fades to be replaced by utter fear, she stares at Byrad a look of terror on her face as she sobs, "I don't know. I don't know!"
Byrad stares at her for a moment, then sheathing his sword he puts his arms around the young thief.
"Do not worry we will find out what is wrong."
Silently he says a prayer for her, knowing that by Élan Vitals will they would solve her problems.

*

Ammaris stares into the huge cavern, its ceiling hung with huge rock formations, its floor strewn with rubble from those that had fallen.

In the flickering torchlight he sees hundreds of Orcs, but this alone is not enough to make him gape. Not even the shimmering veins of gold and silver can distract his gaze, rather it is the group of beings held captive in a large cage.

"Dwarves" Ammaris breathes in awe.

The large group, about forty or fifty sit in miserable exhausted silence, and the sorcerer suspects the captives hope of escape had been beaten and worked out of them.

A group of Orcs approaches the cage, with a snarled command the Dwarves are dragged to the back of the cave. Soon the sounds of hammer and pick echo through the still air.

Ammaris sits back against the rock wondering what he should do, taking a look at the cavern he notices another cage. this one holds the young and old, women and children of the dwarves.

Frowning Ammaris lifts the hood of his green robes and finds a shadowed crevice. He sits and lays his staff down, relaxing he slips into a sorcerer's trance. Soon he looks at himself and his aura of power, seeing it is pale and weak. His gaze goes to the staff it too was fading.

Returning to consciousness the sorcerer closes his eyes then pulls out his book, flipping through the few pages that hold his spells he frowns at his limited choices. Shaking his head he puts the book away again.

Ammaris looks at his empty hands, then down at his staff. Frowning he mutters to himself.

"Do I have a choice?" his only answer is yes, stay and help or leave and maybe forget them all.

He grabs his staff, stands and steps away from the entrance. Stooping he picks up a rock, then stops and murmurs softly.

A soft light forms around the upheld rock, growing and filling with muted colours. Soon the spell is complete and he spins and strides to the cavern.

*

Tammara and Byrad continue their search for Ammaris, room after room, finding a lot of dust but no sorcerers.

Slowly, though, the duo discover used areas. Stepping carefully they walk swept halls and rush-strewn chambers. They step into a hall and Tammara freezes, raising her hand to stop Byrad.

The thief moves to a door and leans close listening. After awhile she steps back drawing her daggers.

"What did you hear?" whispers Byrad.

"Voices, but not speaking the king's tongue, or what we heard the Orcs speaking."

Byrad nods and draws his sword he walks to the door and pulls it open.

The room is a dining hall, a large stone table with oak benches dominates the room. Byrad stares curiously at the furnishings, for they were half as big as normal, though obviously sturdy.

The table holds the remains of a hastily vacated dinner, consisting of surprisingly normal looking, and tasty, food.

Walking to a door opposite they step into another corridor, still no sign of life.

They step forward and Byrad grunts in surprise and looks down as his foot sinks on a stone.

"Don't move!"

To late Tammaras shout comes. As Byrad lifts his foot the stone rises and a click sounds. Dust falls from above and the two of them dive forward as stone drops, blocking the door behind. Then with a grating groan they see a slab of rock lower ahead of them.

Tammara runs and Byrad follows, sprinting he chases the thief, but she stumbles with a curse. Byrad leaps forward, dropping his sword as he gathers Tammara into his arms and propels them both through the door. Sliding across the floor they hear the shuddering stone slam down.

As the dust settles Byrad and Tammara stand. Dusting off his clothes Byrad looks at the now blocked doorway.

"Byrad"

He spins on hearing the tone in her voice, his hand going for the sword that he had dropped in the tunnel.

He reaches for his short sword but as he sees the group before him his hand drops.

About eighty short powerfully built 'men' stand with levelled crossbows. Each sports a beard and is armoured in plate mail. One of the beings steps forward.

Byrad listens distractedly as the being talks, not understanding a word the *Dwarf*, for that was what they were, says.

The dwarf pauses then says, "I asked who you were and what you are doing here."

Byrad nods and then it occurs to him that the dwarf had spoken in the kings' tongue.

"Sorry, I am Byrad, this is Tammara. We are looking for a friend."

The Dwarf places a hand on his belt, "This friend," he says, "where is he?"

Byrad shrugs, "That's the point. He fell down a well above us, we have searched for hours."

The dwarf steps forward, some thing about him other than the crowned helm shows him to be king,

"You have been above." He says with a strange hopeful look in his eyes. "Have you seen any of my kind?"

Byrad shakes his head, "No I am afraid not. The only others we have met have been Orcs."

As the last word leaves Byrads mouth the king's eyes open wide. Suddenly the other dwarves erupt in a frenzy of shouting, and though the humans cannot understand they know the tone: Hatred.

"Now you've done it." Mutters the king, he turns back to his people and attempts to calm them.

Some time later the dwarves were calmer and the king turns back to Byrad and Tammara.

"Byrad, Tammara my people want orc blood. Our kinsmen ruled here and we've come to find them, if there are Orcs then we must kill them and learn the fate of our people. Will you help us?"

Tammara shrugs and Byrad nods, "If it helps us find our friend, we will."

The king nods, "We have been following the traces of our people down wards, I think we travel the same way."

The three grip hands and they head on.

Chapter Twelve

Ammaris stands before the orc chief, and its army. They all have weapons drawn and stare at the human evilly, the limp form of a dwarf child in his hand.

The orc chief and his army step forward muttering, "Yoouz goin' to die human." spits the Orc chief, the others laugh, "Yoouz going to suffer."

Ammaris looks around the cavern, seemingly uninterested in the chiefs statement. He looks back from the shadows of his hood and sneers as he finally answers, "I have a gift *orc*. This dwarf child I found outside the cave. I give it to you."

The chiefs eyes narrow as he stops and reaches out, but freezes as Ammaris smiles cunningly.

"What you want?"

Turning away and walking towards the cage, Ammaris speaks over his shoulder, "I am pleased to see you have great intelligence, equal at least to your brawn." Ammaris smiles as he glances back and sees the orc beaming with pleasure at the flattery, "In exchange for the dwarf I would have supplies and a way out of these infernal caverns." he reaches the cage and waits.

"What if I just kill you?" the orc asks.

Ammaris turns to face the chief and shakes his head, "I don't think you want to do that." He states and murmurs softly. His staff flares into light.

The Orcs snarl in distress and even the chief seems fearful.

"Well?" asks Ammaris.

The chief looks at his minions, then back at the sorcerer, his mind turning over choices. Finally his mind settles on a certainty.

If I attack the human then he will kill me first.

"Ok, sorcerer." says the orc.

Ammaris grins and bows, turning he flings the dwarf illusion into the cage. Coming back to the orc he absently wipes his hand on his robes and begins listing the items he wants.

Ammaris shoulders the pack and heads to the entrance, the Orcs watching him as he leaves. As he reaches the cave mouth he hears a gurgle then a thud. Whirling he sees the orc guarding the dwarves slumped near the cage, one dwarf holding the bloody stone.

The Dwarves scramble out of the cage as the Orcs draw their weapons. The Chief snarls something at Ammaris then drags free his sword and begins to run at the sorcerer.

Ammaris is dimly aware of the dwarves fighting the Orcs, his attention is focused on his magic.

Holding the staff before him he shouts out the words.

The Orc chief skids to a stop as he feels the wind hit him, then the magical forces sweep him up and carry him back to the other Orcs. The dwarves scramble for cover, huddling together as the creatures that had held them are flung against the ancient rock of the cavern.

As the wind dies Ammaris drops to his knees head bowed. The surviving Orcs battered as they are, soon find themselves on the run from the miners, who had streamed from the tunnels armed with pick and hammer. The dwarves attack in a frenzy.

"Human are you all right?" Asks a dwarf laying a hand on Ammaris' shoulder.

Ammaris looks up and sees a dwarf with a blood stained hammer in his hand. Standing Ammaris nods,

"Yes." He gazes at the staff for a moment then adjusts his pack and turns, "Thank you."

The dwarf grabs his arm,

"Wait human, you saved us. We owe you. Come." He grips Ammaris' hand and then heads back to his people. Ammaris watches him go then follows.

*

Byrad, Tammara and the dwarves stride along the passageway. Not too long ago they had heard a roar, followed by a wind that should not be in the caverns.

Byrad had suppressed his hopes, for the wind had made him remember Ammaris' spell.

Suddenly they all stop as the sound of running feet comes to them then, about twenty bloodstained Orcs come from around the corner. With screams of rage the dwarves launch themselves at the creatures. In moments the Orcs are destroyed and the dwarves run down the corridor, they exit the tunnel and meet their kin.

The king walks up to Byrad, "Well lad I think we have found both my people and your friend." He points to the huddled form sat against the wall.

Byrad grins and thanks the dwarf.

Hurrying to Ammaris' side he grabs him in a hug.

"Byrad, I'm glad to see you too!" He exclaims with a laugh.

"How are you?"

The sorcerers eyes cloud for a moment but he grins, "I am fine, just a little chilled." The last is choked off by a cough.

Byrad laughs and slaps his back.

They turn at a commotion and see the Dwarves had gathered a great feast, kegs of ale were rolled out. The two friends look at each other then run for the barrels.

Some time later Ammaris sits near a fire, his staff across his knees and a mug of ale in hand.

"Excuse me, lord." Ammaris looks up to see a young dwarf.

The dwarf holds something in his hands, "My father, the smith, he asked me to give you this."

Ammaris takes the item an old leather bound book, "Thank you." The dwarf nods and walks away.

The sorcerer looks at the book in his hands and reads the word branded on the cover.

ZUKALAM

Ammaris drops the mug he was about to drink from. His eyes go from that one word to the name beneath, *Magri Morcarcion.*

Opening the book he reads the first page.

This is my attempt at reconstructing my fathers work. He has bequest me to continue with my studies, but I have discovered his work is gone.
Hopefully this will keep his discovery alive.

M.M
Creation of sorcery

Ammaris reads the words again, his shaking hands turn the page and he begins to study the most ancient of Sorcery secrets.

Tammara wanders about and sees Byrad talking with a group of dwarves, she walks over just as they depart to the ale and food. Byrad rolls up a piece of parchment and then sees the thief, pushing the scroll into a pouch hung around his neck.
"Tam, have you seen Ammaris?"
Tammara shakes her head and Byrad grins as he says, "How much to bet he is near ale and food?"

Byrad and Tammara find Ammaris slumped over a book. His friend shakes him awake and he looks about sleepily, then quickly puts away the book.
"We are ready to go Amm." says Byrad.
The sorcerer nods and he gets up, draining his flat ale. Coughing softly they prepare to leave, the dwarf king bids them fair journey.
Byrad stops and speaks with the king, and quickly explains their quest.
The dwarf nods, "We know where you need to go."
"What!"
The king turns to his aide and soon a dwarf runs up, "Diam here will show you the way." He turns to Ammaris and bows, "You shall be welcome here, my lord Sorcerer if ever you should return."
With that the three friends turn and follow the dwarf.
He leads them to a dust choked passage. He points down it then bows low and hurries away.
They all look down the tunnel, then Byrad pulls free his short-sword and readies the silver shield and steps forward.

Chapter Thirteen

The trio walk quietly down the passage, after a moment Tammara breaks the silence,

"What do you think we'll find?"

"Hopefully," replies Byrad, "the tomb of my ancestor and the heirloom, the sword that Karmarthen enchanted all those years ago."

Ammaris listens as the other two talk, while he ponders the fact that his ancestor created the sword Byrad wants. If the weapon is what it seems to be, then Byrad will gain one of the few powerful sorcery artefacts created, one of the ancient Rune-blades.

The other two stop.

"What is it?"

Byrad stands still then a gust of chill wind blows past them, the torches gutter then go out.

Ammaris quickly casts a spell and a glow illuminates them. They peer down the passage then press on.

After many hours of hard, hot and claustrophobic travel they walk into a huge cavern, cool after the stifling tunnel. Ammaris' light cannot reach the walls or ceiling, but does show row upon row of open stone coffins.

In the silence they step a little closer to the coffins but fall back with cries of fear. Skeletal warriors sit up and clamber out of their beds, swords in hand armoured and seemingly ready for combat.

Soon the friends are surrounded by corpses, then a gap opens and they see one skeletal warrior step forward.

It is armoured in burnt black plate mail, only the open visor shows its true ivory body, it holds a large sword in one hand. Tarnished as it is from long disuse, the weapon is still deadly the light plays over the faint runes and along the razor edge.

Byrad gazes at the armour his family crest is etched into the breastplate.

"WHO ARE YOU?" the words make them all jump, Byrad clears his throat.

"I am Byrad Branight. I come to claim the sword of my family."

"YOU MUST VANQUISH ME IN BATTLE." Its voice echoes otherworldly.

Byrad glances at the warriors all around as they step back creating a battle ring, then looks at Ammaris and Tammara.

"IF YOU FAIL YOUR COMPANIONS WILL JOIN YOU."

Byrad looks to his friends, when they nod he passes his pack to Ammaris and steps back into a fighting stance.

The clang of sword and shield echoes in the tomb, each combatant tries to find an opening.

Time and again Dynadryds blade strikes out only to be turned aside by Byrads silver shield, sparks fly as the two magic's clash.

Though Byrad has the skills, drilled into him by the best swordsmen his father could find, he was tiring where as his opponent had no such considerations; plus the short reach of his sword put him at a distinct disadvantage.

Byrad stumbles, the blade of his opponent slicing over his head. That stumble Byrad realises had saved his life, but soon even his luck was going to fail, just as his endurance was failing now.

Stepping back away from the skeletal warrior Byrad tries to regain his strength. Surprisingly Dynadryd does not press the young man, he waits while Byrad rests.

"Why do you wait?" Pants Byrad.

"YOU ARE AT A DISADVANTAGE, FOR I DO NOT TIRE. YOU MAY REST WHEN YOU WISH, BUT MAY NOT LEAVE UNTIL VICTORIOUS OR VANQUISHED."

"Here." Ammaris hands Byrad a water skin from which he takes a long pull, the cool water tasting like honey to his parched throat. Byrad looks to his ancestor.

"How long can I rest for?" he asks.

"FOR HOWEVER LONG YOU WISH." It answers coldly.

Byrad sinks to the floor, trying to control his breathing and regain his strength.

"Do you think he can win?" asks Tammara.

Ammaris watches the fight, three times Byrad had stopped to rest but he was loosing this battle.

"Yes... though this Dynadryd was able to defeat beings not of this world."

Tammara looks at Ammaris, "I don't understand."

Ammaris flinches as a sword swipe leaves a line of blood on Byrad's arm.

"I'll get Byrad to explain."

Byrad swings low only to have it clang uselessly off his opponent's armour, not having enough power to even scratch the metal.

The young Branight steps back and the fight pauses, but all Byrad does is drop his shield and grip his sword with two hands, even the short-sword was becoming heavy.

He fights hard but is tiring fast, his body reacts while his mind wanders. In his minds eye he sees Branight, its proud walls cracked. The gates were a twisted ruin. His father...

Byrads head lifts from his stupor, his body shifts and he begins to battle, using skills he had learnt years ago. The tide of the fight had changed, Dynadryd was forced back his weapon used in defence. Byrads anger gives him strength, his churned up emotions keep him going when he would have fallen, he uses the one thing his opponent lacks.

Screaming in rage at the thing holding him from his goal, keeping him from his fathers side, Byrad swings, slashes, hacks and thrusts at Dynadryd, unmindful of his mounting wounds Byrad presses on.

Soon he is covered in blood, he never stops once and then with a scream he bats the sword of Branight to the side.

Byrad swings with all his might and his opponent shows the flaw in Byrads attack. The bloodied priest staggers back as his ancestors blade rips into his side, with a cry Byrad falls. The battle pauses and Ammaris rushes forward, he pulls a flask from his belt and looks to the warrior. It nods once and the sorcerer forces his dying friend to drink.

The potion brings Byrad back from death and slowly the wounds begin to heal. The priest struggles up as the potion flows through him. He bows to his ancestor, then gripping Ammaris' shoulder once he turns back to the fight.

Byrad was still breathing hard as he steps forward and he focuses on one thing: he must win or his friend would die.

Gripping his sword firmly he attacks, this time he watches his opponent. Without true living mobility the warriors actions were slightly stilted. He moves in the classic attack and defences taught in his time, defences that Byrad knew. With almost heavy heart he breaks the defence, and with an ironically classic attack cleaves the head from the skeletal shoulders.

To Byrad the armour falls to the floor in slow motion, then he sags to his knees shaking.

Ammaris and Tammara run to their friends side. Byrad looks up and smiles shakily then he topples over.

Chapter Fourteen

Byrad awakes to find himself propped against the doorway, he looks around vaguely. Ammaris lifts a sliver flask to his lips and Byrad swallows the liquid, his breathing slows and his mind clears. He looks down and sees his body covered in bandages soaked in the same potion and notices Tammara studying the distant doors.

He tries to stand and with Ammaris' help stagers to the remains of his ancestor. Surrounded by the skeletal warriors now still as statues, Byrad reaches down for the sword.

As his hand touches the hilt a surge of strength flows through him, his exhaustion seems to fall away. He stands tall and watches in awe as the runes on the blade flare silver, the tarnish is turned to dust and the blade shimmers, then returns to its normal iron-grey.

The sword was nothing special, made from one piece cast-iron, straight, sharply pointed and dark. Its hand guard spreads from the hilt flat and square, the hilt itself ends in an octagonal counterweight, a rune cut into it.

Byrad looks down at the armour, the body of Dynadryd was gone. Ammaris picks up the helmet, and hands it to Byrad.

"My lord"

Byrad takes the full visor helm, as he does so it reacts the same as the sword the soot flaking off, revealing steel. Ammaris helps Byrad into the ancient armour, beginning to speak as he struggles with a buckle on the breastplate.

"One of the dwarves was telling me that once many years ago, a sorcerer came to their city in these mountains. He asked them to make a suit of armour for a human, they agreed and forged it from a metal unknown to humans at that time. They called it *mithril*, human smiths found it and called it *steel* in later years, though the dwarves said it was not the same."

"And you think this is that armour?" says Byrad adjusting his breastplate.

111

"Yes." Ammaris nods as he steps back.

Byrad pulls on his gauntlet and picks up the sword again, it flares silver as he touches it. Picking up its ivory scabbard he finds it has two silver clasps that clip to the armour.

"Why hasn't it got a normal scabbard?" asks Tammara coming over.

Byrad shrugs but Ammaris frowns as he strokes his goatee, "Byrad, strike the wall."

Byrad laughs, but Ammaris just repeats him self. Frowning thinking his friend mad Byrad half-heartedly swings at the stone, expecting it to bounce off. He is understandably shocked when it slices in with a screech of metal and stone and a chunk of the wall falls to the floor.

"I'd be careful with that if I were you." Ammaris says smugly.

Byrad stares at his friend which only makes his smile broader. The armoured man grabs his old sword and ties it to his pack, which he slings onto his shoulder. Picking up his shield he looks at the still smirking sorcerer, "You know," Byrad says, "you can be extremely annoying."

They turn and head for the doors, stopping when the warriors salute Byrad and return to their coffins. Byrad says a prayer and then they move on.

They come to the 'front door' a large stone affair, Byrad heaves against it and it slowly grinds open. They are nearly blinded by the early summer sunlight that streams into the tomb.

Stepping out into the fresh mountain air they see, after a few moments of blindness, that they stand at the bottom of a trail. Hefting their packs they begin hiking up the trail, Byrad groans causing his companions to laugh mercilessly, high above vultures circle.

*

On the gods plane the deities gather at the centre of that realm, not for twelve hundred years had such a thing happened.

Each god was present. Immoha Sun God was there, dressed in his golden armour his hand clasping a gold glowing morning star.

Corinthia Moon Goddess frees her silver-headed mace; its round head glowing a cold white, she stands silent in her pearly robes.

Zumithia night goddess watches the sun and moon, her fingers brush the black dagger that is thrust into her midnight blue robes.

The next is slim and young looking, dressed in gaudy and bright clothing, a rapier at his side and a grin on his face. Trickster slips about the others annoying the great armoured god.

War swings at Trickster, the only one who could have dodged his blow did so, the Lord of battles checks his weapons. All the weapons of war hang from straps, belts and clasps all over his frame.

Tempest Storm God stands amid a thunder storm, his grey robes shimmer with water and his hand grips a number of copper javelins.

Insitina Agricultural Goddess sits on a patch of green grass, a grain-flail near her green stained knee.

Oceanus stands, a trident in hand his beard dripping from the seas he commands.

The hunting god, Hakim stands away from the two watery gods, keeping the huge bow he leans on dry. He is dressed in leathers of brown and green.

The last is Laumas-Nahtan, Earth God, he leans on his huge maul of stone, his own form armoured in white marble.

The twins stand waiting, the other gods stare at them, some with shadowed fear.

"They have left the tomb." Says Ackza softly, he lifts his weapon, a great scythe. An image of three humans appears, seen through the eyes of one of the death gods minions, one in robes of green, one in armour, one in leather.

They stare at the humans and Tempest disappears with a crash of thunder, the humans are soon drenched with rain and they are running as thunderbolts rip into the mountain.

The gods shake their heads in hopelessness.

Ackza and Élan-Vital point to the fleeing humans,

"See! The new face of chaos." They say, and even their voices crack.

*

The companions flee before the storm, racing ahead of the lightening, covering ears from the thunder.

They spot a cavern, its opening huge and welcoming. Rushing inside they collapse to their knees, but soon head deeper as the lightening strikes the mountain. Boulders soon fill the cave mouth.

In the darkness Ammaris pants deeply, he whispers magic and soon a glow appears.

"Is every one ok?" He asks, they nod and climb to their feet.

Looking around they head in the only direction possible, into the cave. Turning the corner they stop dead, the light from Ammaris illuminates an immense cavern filled with seemingly the worlds riches.

Treasures stretch as far as the eye can see: jewels, silver, gold, weapons and armour are heaped in a carpet of wealth.

Tammara runs forward, she grabs up coins and jewels and begins to stuff her pack. Byrad and Ammaris lean on their knees panting from the run, they marvel at the young thief's stamina.

As they examine the treasure a thought enters each of their minds, *where did this treasure come from, why was it here?*

Byrad and Tammara look up then Ammaris breaks the sudden silence, "Oh shit." The others look round, they see the sorcerer holding a large shield.

"What is it?"

Ammaris looks at his friends and turns the 'shield', they instantly realise their mistake. It was not a shield, it was black, roughly shield shaped but naturally so. A low rumble comes from the far side of the cavern, a huge shadow moves in the dark outside Ammaris' magic. Then they see the owner of the 'shield' come forward: the Dragon.

The companions freeze in fear, and then as the creature opens its mouth they scatter.

Byrad runs unhooking his helm, fitting it he draws his sword the blade flaring white as he grabs up his shield. He turns and sees his companions safe for now, the Dragons attention was on himself.

He has no time to dodge the flame and he lifts his shield in a futile attempt of protection. The flames strike the shield and fan out around it, no heat could Byrad feel. The Dragon roars in anger and Byrad runs at the creature.

114

This is suicide! Byrad says to himself as he runs, but a battle cry escapes his lips.

The Dragons huge head thrusts forward at his shout and Byrad skids to a halt. He is struck by a foul rotting stench, and Byrad sees that the Dragon was not the one that had attacked them before. This Dragon was falling apart and then he realises it was dead, or undead. The Dragon peers at him, at his armour and seems to become furious.

"BRANIGHT!" it roars, "YOU SHOULD HAVE STAYED DEAD. I SHALL HAVE TO BURN YOU AGAIN."

With that the creature rears up and Byrad turns and runs.

Ammaris was fumbling with his pack, and then he grabs the sorcerers tome he had been given so long ago. Flipping through the pages he finds the spell and reads through it, he turns and motions to Tammara.

"What is it sorcerer?" she asks as she comes over, a pair of skull hilted short swords in her hands, they gleam unnaturally.

"Where did you get those?" asks the sorcerer.

Tammara points to a silver and oak case.

"Hmm" Ponders Ammaris studying the weapons, "if this doesn't work we may need any mystical weapons." He hands the girl the tome open at the spell, "Tammara you must keep this still, turn the page when I nod. Understood?"

"Yes"

Ammaris looks back over to the running form of Byrad then he begins.

"VORX CEN ORINSU~" Ammaris pronounces each word carefully. *"Roadhouse, Ó~"* the air crackles with his power, and a sphere of sorcery forms over head. He nods and the page is turned the spell was still stable, with elation he shouts the last words into the gathering magic. *"ELITI, POTANASTAL!"*

Byrad dives under the Dragons talon-swipe, rolling to his knees he looks up as Ammaris finishes the last word. The sphere of sorcery seems to implode, then with a silence that was completely unnatural three shafts of light strike out at the companions.

Byrad sees the Dragons maw bear down on him he ducks expecting to be crushed. Instead he falls through darkness hitting something hard, his helmeted head clangs on stone and the darkness takes him.

Chapter Fifteen

Waking up Byrads first thought is how much pain he is in. His body feels like it had been pulled and stretched to the limit, opening his eyes he stares up into the night sky, stars twinkle high above.

Sitting up he sees two lumps nearby, seeing his sword at his side he picks it up to sheath it, but it flares into silver light. He moves to his friends side and sees Tammara come around.

"Ow!" she says as she sits up.

"You all right?" asks Byrad lifting his visor.

"Apart from feeling like I've been on the rack for a life time? Yes I am." Her gaze drops to Ammaris and they see his face is pale and still, his staff in hand.

"Ammaris" Byrad shakes his friend, but gets no reaction.

"Why don't you pray?"

"I can't not until my God has a Church, he has not enough power on this world, his healing has been given from his own essence." He looks around and sees that they are on a road he recognised and just north he could see the light of the inn.

"Come on help me get him to the inn."

"What about his clothes?"

Byrad curses, he knew the owner would help but the patrons would not understand.

"We'll go around the back."

They reach the shadowed rear of the inn and Byrad opens the back door. A startled woman steps back hand on a large cooks knife, but upon seeing Byrads burden she quickly helps.

"We will put him in his room." She guides them to a small room set at the back.

Byrad sees it is filled with books and scrolls obviously Ammaris' home away from home. They lay him on a bed and the woman begins to examine the sorcerer, efficiently checking him for wounds, fever or any thing else.

"Find my husband and get your selves rested, you can't do anything here."

The woman shoos them out into the hall and they leave, entering the inn through the front.

Evad greets Byrad warmly but on seeing his face he ushers them up to a twin room.

"What's happened?" he asks when the door is shut.

Byrad takes off his helm and begins working on his armour, noticing for the first time it is splattered with Dragons blood.

"Ammaris is not well, we owe him our lives and can not help him." Byrads voice is heavy with exhaustion and hopelessness.

Evad comes over and helps him with his armour, and he tries to lighten the mood.

"I see you've improved your travelling attire." Byrad looks at the man and smiles slightly, soon though he is abed and asleep. The innkeeper shows Tammara to her room and promises to check on their mutual friend.

*

Élan-Vital feels the pain of his high priest. He gathers himself and goes to him in his dreams, promising his friends survival and telling him the way to bring this about.

*

Byrad awakes the next morning refreshed and full of hope. He had received word from his god, about how he could save his friend and return his deity to the world of men.

He meets Tammara and tells her of his plan over breakfast, then checks on Ammaris and while he is no better he is also no worse.

Soon the duo are prepared for travel once again, Tammara had agreed to go with Byrad to help him. She returns to her room and gathers her pack and weapons.

The thief belts on the skull hilted swords and turns to leave, but suddenly she is assaulted by pain in her head. The voice that had been silent for so long she had forgotten it, speaks to her.

"Go kill the sorcerer he is our enemy kill him!"

"No. Please he is my friend."

"Kill him!"

Tammara stands as the voice echoes in her mind, repeating the words over and over. She shoulders her pack and slips into Ammaris' room. Pulling her swords and gazes at them then she shivers as the door opens and Byrad walks in.

"What is it Tammara?" he asks hand on sword as he looks around the room.

118

"Nothing I...I was just remembering Ammaris said these were mystical, but he never told me in what way. He didn't have a chance." She slides them back into the black sheaths.

Byrad puts his hand on her shoulder and promises they will save him.

As they leave Tammara wonders who would save her.

*

Six naked captives kneel before the throne of Branight, on the blood stained desecrated altar of Laumas-Nahtan. The three men and three women bow their heads in fear and horror, the creature gazes at them hungrily. He turns to Amryd stood beside the throne that had been his.

"Amryd, has the armour been prepared?"

The vampire bows, "Yes Great-one." He claps his hands and the armour is laid before the captives.

The creature stands and steps to the prisoners, he raises them to their feet.

"You are honoured to be my servants," he states his hands running over their bodies, he gestures to the armour and they shake in fear. The armour rises from the floor and crackles with chaotic power, the six humans are soon screaming in agony as the armour bonds to them. The creature returns to its throne and laughs as he watches them writhe.

*

The duo travel north-east along the Branight road, a few glance at the symbol Byrad displays. Ignoring them all they keep moving towards his home.

His thoughts are in turmoil, he has the sword he needed, he has the fate of a god on his shoulders and the life of his friend resting on his success. He knew how to accomplish the tasks: Kill his father, destroy the creature and pray at the altar thus changing the Church-palace from one god to another.

Tammara walked beside Byrad actually enjoying the sunshine, and the walk. She had not 'heard' from the voice since that morning, and she hoped she would not hear it again.

At the end of a long day of travel, they make camp before the last stint of the journey to the city. They eat a healthy meal of fruits, meats and bread washed down by ale and water.

119

Byrad breaks the night-time silence after the meal, "We should head off early tomorrow morning and reach the city by midday. Are you still happy to join me?"

Tammara nods, "I want to help. You can't go it alone and even with two of us it is a chancy thing."

They talk for awhile longer deciding on their best chance of success. Then they turn in for the night, Tammara standing first watch.

Tammara watches the darkness as Byrad sleeps and she listens to the night sounds. Getting up she patrols a perimeter around the camp. As she is about to return to her companion she hears a sound nearby and creeps towards it. She relishes the feeling that using her skills gives her, she had not done this on her own for a while and she needed the practice. She creeps up to a low wall and peers over it, what she sees makes her duck back down. Even in the darkness she knew the sight of a troll.

It was chewing on what looked like a cow. She shudders with fear and then draws her swords, she owed these creatures something.

Climbing over the wall she stalks her target keeping down wind she comes up to its back and, hisses.

"Die!" the creature stands and whirls but taken completely by surprise it has no chance. Tammara thrusts with both blades and the creature roars once then is dead, black light erupts through it and along the swords.

Tammara gasps and throws back her head as the magic flows through her, and a dark light erupts from her small frame.

Byrad awakes and draws his sword in a blaze of silver light, a roar had awaked him. Now he hears a sound he recognises, Tammara in pain. "AHHHH"

Racing for the sound he leaps the wall, seeing Tammara slumped within a smouldering and scorched patch of earth.

Walking to his friends huddled form, he looks at the devastation that stretches in a circle from the wall to about ten meters around her. Grabbing her up with one arm he caries her back to camp.

Carefully he tries to take her blades but her fingers would not release. Byrad builds up a fire and sheaths his glowing sword, he watches over another friend in trouble.

Next morning just as the sun rises Tammara awakes, she looks around and stretches.
"Good morning!" she says.
Byrad looks at her and nods,
"Morning, what happened last night?" he asks.
The thief shrugs an apology,
"I'm sorry I must have fallen asleep on watch. More tired than I thought." She sees Byrads eyebrows raise, "Look I'm sorry it won't happen again."
Unconvinced Byrad asks, "How do you feel?"
"Truth to tell I've never felt better, I could take on anything."
Byrad nods and hands her bread and cheese, he watches her as she eats. She seemed fine, but he could not shake off a feeling of unease. Frowning he shakes his head, mentally pushing the thoughts from his mind. Not long after a quick breakfast they head off, making good time as they come into sight of the city just before midday.
Tammara gasps at the devastation of the city ruin, "You lived *there*?"
Byrad nods and wanders over to a hedgerow concealing his pack, he dons his helm and shield and heads for the city. Drawing his sword it flares silver, bright even in the noon glare. Tammara hides her pack and runs after him.

*

Byrad and Tammara head into the city and edge towards the Church palace.
This was the place Byrad knew his father and the creature would be. Curiously they saw nothing, undead or otherwise. They reach the Church and Byrad looks to Tammara she nods and draws her blades.
They enter the dark interior of the Church and strain to see through the dark, oily mist filling the building. Walking forward Byrad becomes aware of something else in the Church, something powerful and evil. Byrad and Tammara freeze as a hideous scream fills the foul air, shivering they cower. Byrad remembers his Gods promise and Ammaris' reliance on his

success, he looks at Tammara she nods and they press on.

They walk through the mist and Byrad trips on something. Crouching down he dimly sees a skeletal body dressed in the armour of the Church guards, he sees more remains as the mist swirls away.

Reaching one wall they look about trying to see in the darkness, the large door to the throne and altar room looms before. Stepping over to it they recoil as they see hanging from the door a humanoid body, it was striped, not naked but striped of skin. The body shivers and they stumble back retching.

With hideously slow movement it raises its head and screams once in horrifying pain, then its head falls forward again. The door opens beckoning them inside.

They step forward and feel the power closer now, stopping in the entrance to the huge room gagging on the foul mist which is even thicker here.

Byrad feels the mist draining all warmth from him, his attention is focused on moving forward, Tammara at his back. He reaches the centre of the room and the mist swirls away, he stands coughing and looks up, on the throne he sees the creature. It lounges with feet on the altar, which is covered in bloody remains and simply watches him. He looks around and sees that Tammara is gone, and then a scream the same as from the door sounds from the left. He turns and sees masses of flesh piled at the sides of the room, fleshy faceless heads rise with that one and he is nearly deafened by the screams of pain. Byrad sags to his knees his head bowed and eyes tearing with sorrow.

"The underlings of your priestly father welcome you." the creature calls out.

Tammara hides behind a pile of flesh, her body shakes, she knows the creature before her friend, recognising it as if it were her own reflection. Anger boils away the fear and she waits for the right moment.

Through blurry pain filled eyes Byrad looks upon the creature, and his father at its side. Standing he advances through the screams and heads first for the creature.

Amryd claps his hands and six armoured figures, much like the one in the throne, step from the shadows. The faces he recognises, these were his fathers guards, his friends.

They rush at him and he defends himself against their armoured talons.

Tammara creeps along the wall, soon she is soaked in the blood of priests but she heads for the creature. The voice was urging her on and amid the ruined Church she listens. She sees Byrad fighting for his life one of the creatures erupting in silver light, turned to dust by the sword, and then another is gone from a sweeping back hand swipe. The creature she was after was not enjoying the show and it stood ready to destroy Byrad itself.

With a scream she runs at it and as it turns to see her, the creature screams in fear. She hacks and slashes at the thing, the magic of her swords ripping the life from it. Suddenly the creature splits apart and a great oozing mass of blackness rears up.

Byrad sees Tammara attacking the creature, as he dispatches the two remaining warriors. Turning to help her he sees Amryd suddenly race towards him.

Twisting he tries to evade his father but the creature gleefully lays his hand on his son. Byrad feels the evil touch even through his armour, he feels his body relax and his mind cloud, with his last thought he prays.

Amryd screams and a stench of burning flesh sears into Byrads nose, he shakes his head and steps back as his father clasps a scolded hand. The vampire hisses at Byrad and draws his sword, its blade as black as night. "Your faith will not stop me, son." Amryd waves his sword about, "My *master* gave this to me when I surrendered your mother to him. It will, I think, be enough to kill you." Amryd swings the sword and Byrad parries it away, black sparks spray from the blade, but Amryd attacks again and again.

Byrad is forced to retreat, defending himself from the blows with sword and shield. Byrad realises his father could not be saved, he *had* chosen his fate. As he realises the truth he releases the love he had had for his father and steps forward into battle.

Amryd sees his sons expression change, then he is forced to defend himself as Byrad begins to attack. Amryd grins and fights back, both well trained but

Byrad was mortal, he would die. He would feel the horror of his blood being drained, sucked dry by his own father.

Amryd blocks a strike and his other hand snaps forward, thundering into Byrads chest. The armour hisses at the unholy touch and buckles as Byrad is lifted from his feet.

"You see!" shrieks Amryd, "*This* is my power, you should join me."

Byrad shakes his head and staggers to his feet, his helm on the floor he advances again sword held ready.

Amryd sneers, "You are as stubborn and weak minded as your mother." Byrad strides closer, "Your mother screamed for a long time, I can almost hear her now."

"After my master had finished he let me have her. I did what I wished to her, and with my new power I could do many things." He looks over to the remains on the altar.

Byrad stagers and his eyes tear at the words, and then the vampire begins to laugh. Byrad throws down his shield and runs at the creature, screaming in hatred.

The vampire dodges a savage blow, designed to sever his head and his own sword sweeps out slashing into Byrads side.

His armour slices open and he drops to the floor, Byrad knew he was dying. Amryd reaches down and drags him up, kicking his sword away it lands near the throne.

"Son, I shall savour this." The vampire casts his son hard to the floor and Byrad groans and coughs up blood, Amryd kneels and pulls Byrads head back. He sinks his fangs into his sons neck, but Byrad wrenches away ripping his neck from the vampire.

"You only prolong the inevitable." Amryd says as Byrad crawls away, the vampire stands and follows him. Byrad moves past his sword and Amryd asks puzzled, "What are you doing, I never thought you were a coward." He stops, pondering, then his eyes widen.

Byrad drags himself forward, inch by inch, he would die soon but he had to go forward a little more, reach the end of his quest and bring Life to so many.

The pain was terrible, his lungs bubble with blood and it drips from his mouth, he hears the vampires

question and smiles as it shouts in horror, too late it understands.
Byrad stops and reaches out...

Amryd races forward in desperation

... And touches the altar, and with his last breath utters a prayer.

*

The god of life suddenly bursts into radiant light, his home among the gods' flares to life and his powers gather to him and in a flash he is gone.

*

Byrad is bathed in the light of his god, his wounds heal and he feels the power flow throughout the Church and the city. He knows the people that had been turned undead were free, returned to the life that had been stolen from them.
The vampire screams and disappears
Then Byrad feels a sharp pain as the power touches Tammara, realising what had been happening to the girl and why.
Tammara turns away and screams in pain as the power of his god bathes her, she flees the Church and the hateful power.

"Byrad"
He turns at his name and sees his god in his mundane form, a tall strong man dressed in simple plate mail armour, silvery and emblazoned with his symbol on the chest plate. His face is of a middle aged man and he has long hair under an open helm.
"You have succeeded. Your friend is returned to you."
Byrad bows low,
"Lord. What of Tammara?"
"She is gone, has been fading for along time. And you know what must be done about her."
Byrad nods and feels his gods hand on his shoulder. Then he is alone.
He stands and feels a touch on his arm, turning he looks down into the face of his mother, crying with joy he hugs her tight. They leave the Church of Élan-vital and step out into a city full of life; a city of hope.

*

Tammara heads northward her mind twisted by both light and dark, her body scarred by the power of Byrads God.

Her warped, pain wracked mind focuses her hurt on *him*.

Her hatred twists within, and her souls twist with it. *He* would suffer, they would all suffer.

*

The Gods stand at the centre of their realm, each one sinks to the ground in fear as they feel the presence on the world, weak but not powerless.

PART TWO: HOPE
(June 21st: Midsummer Day 1236)

Chapter Sixteen

Byrad and Ammaris stand atop the walls of the palace and gaze out over Branight, to the sorcerer it looked as if the entire populous was out helping to rebuild the city. At the north gate teams of workers were building new fortifications. To the south the old gates were being replaced, and all across the city repair work was being carried out.

"I see you have taken the words of your god seriously." States Ammaris leaning forward and studying the work being done.

Byrad glances at his friend, it had been three months since he had appeared at the gates, looking healthy and well. But Byrad had also noticed a slight change in the sorcerer, as if his experience had affected him deeply, though not physically.

"Indeed. Hopefully all of us will heed His words."

"Hmm" Ammaris turns as he hears foot steps approaching, a priest of life, one of the many that had joined the new religion, when their city was delivered from the hands of Amryd and his master. Ammaris steps away from the priest drawing his robes more closely about himself, he leans on his staff and looks out over the wall.

"My Lord Byrad," Says the priest hurrying up, "We have a report from the scouts."

Byrad turns to the priest, "What news?" he asks eagerly.

The priest shakes his head, "I am sorry to say that another has been killed."

Byrad sits back on the wall, it was the third such report he had heard he should have expected it.

Ammaris steps reluctantly closer to the priest, "Was it an accident?" he asks softly. The man shakes his head and suppresses a sob. The sorcerer bows his head and looks at Byrad, he was staring blankly at the stones at his feet. Ammaris dismisses the distraught priest and looks out over the city.

"Byrad call them home." He says, "They are not able to stand against Tammara."

Byrad looks at his friend, "I know that but we must have news of when she will strike. Without that report we have no chance."

Ammaris nods, "Call them back, Byrad. I shall speak with my people and get some aid."

"Do you really think they will listen to you?" Byrad tries to suppress his hope, for with the sorcerers helping the scouts could go undetected in the north, it would stop the deaths and give them a valuable advantage.

The sorcerer shakes his head, "Probably not, already I have broken with tradition and reveal my self as a sorcerer. Add to that the fact I have left my Apprenticeship. They may not even see me."

Ammaris turns to the stairs and leaves, adding, "If they will not help, I shall. You have my promise on that."

The sorcerer pauses at the stairs and steps back as a number of priests' hurry up to the wall.

Byrad watches his friend leave and sighs. He could see his friend was having a difficult time, accepting the fact that his life was due to the intervention of a God. By his reaction to the priests Ammaris was obviously not ready to accept them as his saviours. Byrad shakes off his thoughts and directs the priests to recall the remaining scouts.

As the priests leave him on the walls the lord of Branight looks out over the city. It had been unofficially renamed. The City of Hope it was being called now, his people were sure they would survive. *He* was not so sure, and it plagued him incessantly. Turning away from the view he walks down to the palace proper.

Entering the courtyard Byrad nods to his two bodyguards, he had told them he did not need guards in the city, but they would not listen to him and followed him everywhere. Byrad walks to his palace and all around priests light torches and lanterns, the sun was setting on midsummer day and Byrad was tired. Entering his room, the guards post themselves at his door, he undresses and climbs into bed. He prays to his god and soon falls into a deep sleep.

By the third night Byrad was worried, Ammaris had been gone far longer than the priest had expected. Bidding goodnight to his guards he walks into his bedchamber and sits at his desk, it was littered with papers: notes, estimates from masons and requisitions from the growing army, every thing that made the rebuilding of Branight possible.
As the light grows dim he lights a lantern, but soon he feels his eyes drooping and he goes to his bed. Almost instantly he falls asleep.

Byrad awakes to a commotion outside his door, it was dark but the dawn was sending dim light into the room. He calls out as he grabs a robe and his sword. Opening his door he sees the two guards stood above a huddled form a bag lays next to it. The stranger was dressed in dark red robes but as Byrad reaches the group he smells the iron-rust scent of blood. The robes were shredded and soaked, they glisten wetly as one guard turns the body over.
"Ammaris!" Byrads gasp of shock makes the other guard turn,
"My Lord."
Byrad pushes the men aside and opens his friends saturated robes he sits back, shocked. Ammaris' body was ripped and slashed and covered in blood. The sorcerer groans and Byrad quickly prays over him and soon the wounds heal and Ammaris' breathing eases.
Byrad turns to the guards and orders them to carry Ammaris into his room as they lay him down he asks what had happened.
"My lord," begins one, "He just appeared. One moment the hallway was empty the next he was led where we found him."
Byrad nods and orders water brought to him.
As the guard leaves, the sorcerers arm dangles over the side of the bed, and a piece of wood drops to the floor. Byrad picks it up and realises it was once Karmarthens staff.

Some hours later Byrad watches his friend, Ammaris stirs and awakens, he sits up and looks about.
"Byrad?" asks Ammaris.
The priest smiles and moves to the bed, "How are you?"

Ammaris closes his eyes and leans back, "I am fine, now. What happened?"

"I thought you could answer that. You appeared out side my door nearly dead bloodied as if from a massive fight."

Ammaris nods and asks for water, taking a sip he looks at Byrad, "The sorcerers can't help us."

Byrad stands and curses, "Why? Are they frightened?"

"No."

Byrad turns back to his friend, "What then?"

"They are dead." Says Ammaris softly.

Byrad sits on the bed, "Dead?" he asks, "how?"

Ammaris puts the glass down and stares at it.

Slowly he begins to talk.

"I told you I would get help from the sorcerers, when I got there the place was littered with bodies, my colleagues and friends were ripped apart like rag dolls. I stood horrified and didn't see the creatures. Then as I made my way through the devastation I saw them, or rather they saw me."

Ammaris looks up at Byrad and the priest sees horror and fear, terrible fear in his friends eyes, "They were beasts of some sort. They were feeding, Byrad, *Feeding* on my people." The sorcerer bows his head at the memory and he begins sobbing uncontrollably.

After a moment he continues,

"They saw me and I destroyed the first lot, then I ran. All night they hunted me and I could do nothing, with my power diminished I could not leave. Slowly over the hours my power returned to me and I could have left, but you need sorcery Byrad, we all do and with my people gone I alone can give it. But my power is limited so I crept through the complex and into the masters area, here is kept the artefacts created by sorcerers. I took all I could." He glances at the bag on the table. "I don't know what there is that can help I will need to study them." He falls silent then continues, "I tried to leave then but the creatures found me, I could not battle them without loosing the power to leave, but I had no choice. My staff broke and I ran.

"For the next two days they hunted me, then they stopped. I made my way to the one place I could have teleported from, they were waiting for me. I used what little power I had to spare and fought them off, but they were too much and overwhelmed me. I thought I would die. As they ripped into me and began to feed I heard a voice shout out, the creatures turned and I saw my master. He was bloody and his left leg was a mangled stump, then as the creatures advanced on him he attacked those with his sorcery, three were stopped but the rest overwhelmed him. As I crawled to the teleport room I could hear his screams."

Ammaris stares at nothing as he finishes then he looks to Byrad, his friends face is ashen and he bows his head and prays, Ammaris shakes his head and lays down soon he is asleep again.

Byrad stands and leaves his friend and walks out into the corridor. The two guards stand to attention. as Byrad walks past he sees that they had heard the story, and the soldiers' faces were wet with tears they could not suppress.

The next day Ammaris was awake and well, he sat at the table in Byrads room eating a huge breakfast.

"I see you are better." Says Byrad as he walks in.

Ammaris smiles briefly as he finishes a mouthful.

"Yes I feel... better." Says the sorcerer, he walks to the bed and picks up his bag. "Byrad I will need somewhere to study in peace and quiet." The priest nods and smiles.

"I have the perfect place. Follow me."

The two walk from the room and Byrads two guards follow at a discreet distance, as they see Ammaris they salute. The sorcerer nods once and smiles.

As they walk up a flight of stairs Byrad looks at his friend.

"Ammaris why could you not leave until you reached that one room?"

Ammaris' face visibly pales at the memories and Byrad suddenly regrets asking, the sorcerer stares straight ahead as he answers, "The Complex is protected by sorcery to stop any one from entering except through the teleport room, and that room has spells that would stop any that are not sorcerers from surviving." He looks at Byrad as they reach the top of the stairs and shakes his head as Byrad opens his mouth, Ammaris interrupts, "I do not know how the Beasts got there."

Byrad shuts his mouth and opens the door before them. Ammaris gasps as they step into a brilliantly lit study, books cover shelves on the left but on the right the wall is made up from three huge windows, the middle one has a door that leads to a balcony. Above their heads lots of smaller windows make up the ceiling.

"This was once my fathers private study, through the door ahead is a small bed chamber." Byrad turns to his friend and smiles, "This is your study now."

Ammaris is amazed but he walks to the desk set facing the central window, feeling surprisingly at home,

"I couldn't Byrad." he says without much conviction his gaze travelling over the thousands of books.

"Yes you could." Says Byrad grinning. "If you are to help us then you will need a place of peace and quiet."

Ammaris grabs Byrads hand and shakes it,

"Thank you!"

Byrad claps the sorcerer on the back and closes the door on his way out.

Ammaris opens the doors to the balcony and steps out into the sunshine, his mind racing with plans.

*

Byrad walks into the throne room, already there were people waiting for him. He stops at the altar and prays, then forcing a smile he walks to his throne and sits. As he settles himself he asks his aide to read out the names of those that were waiting.

"The Master Armourer, Captain of Arms, Clerk of Supplies, Master Treasurer..." the list goes on and on then Byrad begins.

Byrad leans back as the meeting finally comes to a close. It was past noon and he was starving, watching as the men and women leave he smiles as the Treasurer passes by, *she* was very pleasing to the eye. Byrad shakes his head and chuckles to himself, and then he calls out to the Armourer.

As the man walks back to the throne Byrad sees the easy way the man caries his huge bulk, muscle upon muscle, plus he has the unmistakable glint of intelligence already shown in his dealings with the merchants flooding the city since the rebuilding began.

"Yes my Lord?" his voice is quiet, but deep.

Byrad turns to his aide and takes from him a roll of parchment. Walking to a table near the throne his aide places a plate of bread and cheese, a tankard of ale and two mugs.

As Byrad reaches the table he passes the parchment to the smith, beginning to devour some of the bread and cheese. After a moment he pours two ales and turns to the man.

"Well?" says Byrad as he hands the man one mug, he glances at it, drains it and stares back at the parchment.

"My lord, this is most impressive, the designs are perfect and as for this formula for an alloy. Where did it come from?"

Byrad smiles, "Can you do it?" he says ignoring the question.

The smith nods, "Yes, how many sets?"

Byrad shrugs as he fills their mugs, "That is unknown as yet, but an armies worth. How long would you need for each?"

The bear of a man begins to pace as he thinks stopping to swig from his mug, then he turns, "One week. Each."

Byrad frowns but nods,

"Ok, begin as soon as possible. The supplies have already been delivered to your shop." Byrad picks up his mug and walks to a side room, his study. He motions for the man to follow and he sits as more food is brought in along with ale. The smith begins to ask questions and the two spend much of the afternoon deep in conversation.

*

Late in the evening Byrad walks slowly back to his room, his thoughts on the new responsibilities he had gained; not only was he the head of the new order of Life, he was also the lord of Branight. On top of this he was attempting to rebuild the city to withstand an impending attack from an army of unknown strength.

As he reaches his room his thoughts are interrupted by the sound of frantically rung bells up on the North wall. Snatching up his sword he belts it on as he, and his two guards race back to the court yard and up to the North wall. Pounding up the steps he sees the guards on the wall staring out over the north road to the grasslands. Joining his men he follows their gaze, in the distance he sees three horsemen race across the bridge over The Lake of Night, the northern most part of his lands. Behind them come three large creatures, steadily gaining on the riders, the scouts from the north.

Byrad turns to the captain of his guards,

"Can we help them? Use the catapults?" he motions to the newly constructed weapons at each end of the wall.

"No my lord," says the man watching the approaching group, "They are moving to fast and we could hit our men."

Byrad looks northward and curses, he glances at the captain and shrugs in response to his stare.

"Is there any thing we can do?"

The man nods and orders bow men to the wall. Byrad leans forward and shudders as the creatures catch one horseman. The rider and mount disappear in a burst of blood and a mass of heaving flesh as the creatures devour the hapless horseman. The others race on.

Ammaris stands at the closed doors of the balcony looking north, he shakes uncontrollably and his reflection in the window is pale. He now knew who was responsible for the deaths of his friends, the genocide of his people.

The Sorcerer looks down at the piece of wood in his hand, the shattered remains of his ancestors staff. He was lucky to have learnt some of the spells held within the staff, before he broke it during his fight with the creatures. He shudders at the memory. Pushing open the doors he steps forward as the creatures give chase again.

The Man on the lead horse leans close over his mounts neck, urging it on. He risks a glance behind and sees the creatures closing on his companion, he looks at the others face and they lock eyes briefly.

The Man sees the resignation and fear drop away as the Other drags on the reins, Turning his horse. Drawing his sword the Other waits, and as his horse is slashed from under him he launches himself at the creatures hacking and slashing. Within seconds he is gone in a spray of blood.

The Man turns his gaze back to the city gates, fear making him cry as his colleague is devoured.

Byrad sees the rider turn back to the creatures, he prays for the mans soul and watches in horror as the man is ripped apart. Looking away he sees Ammaris step out onto his balcony, from his hand he lets something fall, then he begins to cast a spell. Byrad looks back to the last rider and sees the creatures racing after him again, their second meal finished.
The Lord of Branight turns and races from the wall, dragging his sword free it flares into silver light, and again he feels the boost of vitality. He screams for the gates to be opened and forces himself to run, to move faster.

Ammaris utters the words of the spell with barely suppressed anger and hatred,
"*HYLNOR-OROX~*" the magic sparks at his fingertips, his emotions slipping free.

The Man sees the gates opening and he begs the horse to greater speed, the beast labours onwards its great lungs straining. The Man begins to believe he would make it.
Suddenly he is pitched forward to crash hard to the ground, his horse falls next to him as it finally gives its life for its master.
The Man looks to city and sees he is but a hundred meters from the now open gates the soldiers scream at him to get up. He scrambles to his feet and sees the creatures bearing down on him, he races away his only thought is not to die. He stumbles but gets up and races on.
Byrad sees the man racing towards him, sees the creatures stop and devour the horse, then one chases after the grounded rider. Byrad races forward but he knows he would not reach the man, knew with a cold certainty.
He glances up at Ammaris, he was still casting Byrad did not know if the Sorcerer would finish in time, he was not sure if Ammaris knew either.

Ammaris sees the man stumbling forward, the other creatures join in the chase,
"*TRIMORIATA Ó~*" the words are shouted, the magic burns.

The Man stumbles and hears the creatures' blood lust in their roar, crying he stands, the men at the gates urging him to run. The Man turns his back on the castle and faces the creatures. He drags free a throwing axe from his belt and looks up as the Beasts come forward slowly, almost unsure of his intentions now he had stopped running.

Byrad sees the creatures advance on the scout and he curses, he hears the order for the bowmen and the creatures are peppered with shafts, they just keep coming forward oblivious.

Ammaris shakes with emotion and tries to control himself.

The Man watches the creatures approach, they were covered in thick blood coloured fur. He knew with terror he was going to die.
The lead monster rears back and the Man hurls his axe and watches as it slams into the lead creatures' chest.
It rips the weapon free and casts it down at the Mans feet, looking up from the axe the man stumbles back then he hears a scream from above. The Creatures look up and roar in hatred. The Man turns and runs.

Byrad skids to a stop as he hears the scream from Ammaris.

"*TOLMI*" Ammaris screams out the word of sorcery and he feels the hate and anger flow from him, the air before him flickers and burns then with a rumble of sympathetic anger the sorcery flashes forward the air hisses as it passes. Then the creatures' roar is silenced as the sorcery slams into them with explosive force.

Byrad is thrown back as the sorcery slams into the creatures. Pushing himself to his feet he sees a huge cloud of dust outside the city, and a figure staggering through the gates. Rushing forward he sees the Man fall to his knees, he helps him to his feet and they look back as the dust clears and a huge crater is revealed before the city, at the bottom are the remains of the three creatures.

Both men look up and they see Ammaris stager into his room.
The Man turns to Byrad and bows,
"Thank you my Lord." he says pulling away from the helping hand, but then his eyes glaze and he falls into Byrads arms.

Chapter Seventeen

Byrad looks up as the Man awakens with a start, he moves to the bedside and lays a hand on the mans shoulder,
"Don't worry, you're safe."
The Man lies back, "My lord," he croaks, Byrad hands him a cup of water after a sip he starts again. "My Lord, I have important news for you."
Byrad nods.
"Yes, but you are weak." He says softly, "It has been three days since your flight. I shall have some food brought to you, and once you have eaten we shall talk." Byrad raises a hand, "Take time to think on your report, make sure you forget nothing." The man nods and lies back.
"Lord, what of the Sorcerer I would like to thank him."
Byrad pauses at the door,
"I will let him know." Byrad opens the door and steps out, closing it he stops and sighs. Ever since Ammaris had destroyed the creatures the sorcerer had locked himself away in his rooms, and had only opened the door for his meals. Byrad had seen him only once in three days, and his friend was preoccupied and did not speak much. Byrad walks back to his own rooms and does not see a man move to the door.

The man looks up as the door opens and watches as the sorcerer slips in, who looks at the man and smiles briefly,
"Good to see you are well."
"Thanks to you, sir."
Ammaris steps forward, the man had a weathered appearance but he was only in his mid-twenties. His eyes were brown, as was his hair, which he wore in a long ponytail. He was not a large man, but his shoulders were broad and his body toned though not overly muscled. Ammaris turns and looks out the window. It was past midday the sun was high over head, he glances at the walls and notes the guards manning them still looked nervous.
"Ahem!"

Ammaris turns at the discreet cough and looks at the man,
"What?"
"Um, how can I help you?" asks the man again.
Ammaris drags over a chair and sits, "My name is Ammaris." the sorcerer says holding out his hand.
The man shakes it,
"Torran." he says introducing himself.
Ammaris looks out the window again, his thoughts obviously elsewhere, then he shakes his head,
"Torran, will you tell me what you found in the north?"
The man frowns, "I should tell my Lord Byrad first."
Ammaris nods, but his eyes narrow, "You haven't told him yet then."
"No. He said for me to ensure I forget nothing."
Ammaris leans back in his chair and scratches his goatee, then leaning forward he says softly,
"Tell me. I need to know what Tammara is doing."
Torran stares at the sorcerer and sees something in his eyes that he himself recognises: fear. He nods and begins to speak.
"Tammara has taken over the command of an army which is attacking the Kingdom of Erandor. She has changed the soldiers."
Ammaris stands and walks to the window.
"Explain." He says a shiver in his voice.
"She ordered the general into a tent and after about four hours he emerged. He was huge. When he entered he was big, but after he was eight-foot tall and his body a mass of muscle, but also covered in thick dark fur. He ordered his soldiers into the tent and soon they were changed, each time they came out different. Some were seemingly warped, twisted..." he struggles to find the words to describe what he had seen.
Without turning Ammaris murmurs,
"Chaotic."
"Yes! Chaotic" Torran looks at Ammaris and sees him open the window, he continues "After a day those who had been changed were sent to attack the first of three forts that had been holding against the army. The defenders fought well but the, chaos-soldiers." He pauses but the term fitted well. "The Chaos-soldiers seemed not to care if they were injured and it seemed as if they were not easily harmed anyway. I saw a few

139

go down, and these were hacked to pieces. The defenders suddenly found they were on the retreat. As I scouted around I was found and brought before Tammara." Torrans voice fades and Ammaris looks over, he could see the man was pale and sweating.

"What is it?" he asks softly.

Torran looks up and sees the sorcerer looking at him with understanding.

"She told me that she would kill me, but slowly." He laughs bitterly, "She did not realise her first words were the ones I..." he smiles wryly, "...feared most. I wrenched free of the guards holding me and drew my sword, she did not feel my weapons would be a threat." He glances over at a near by table, on it is a wide leather shoulder harness. It holds a basket hilted broadsword at the back and two daggers at the chest; the normal weapons of a scout but also has a double-edged throwing axe on the right hip, the one he had used against the creature at the gate.

Ammaris walks over and studies the weapons, "She was right I assume?" he asks.

"Yes, I hacked and slashed at the chaos-soldiers but could only force them away, as they fell back I ran she laughed and I heard her release those demons. I grabbed a horse and tried to escape."

Ammaris looks at the man and finishes for him, "That is when you rode back here?"

Torran nods and lies back into the pillows. Ammaris glances at the scout and raises his eye brows questioningly the man frowns and shrugs at the supposed question, "I am a coward. In any fight I have ever been in I have tried to run. It is only when I have no chance of escape I stand my ground."

Ammaris nods.

"To me it sounds as if you're simply very sensible: Run if you can, fight if you must." The sorcerer walks back to his chair and moves it back to the table, "Thank you Torran." He opens the door and hurries past a startled servant carrying a tray of food.

Some time later Torran stands before Byrad and waits while his lord ponders the report he had just given. Ammaris stands near the throne dressed in his dark-green robes. Two guards stand near by. Torran studies them, one was short with blue eyes, long straw coloured hair falls to his shoulders mixing with his mutton chop sideburns. His companion-at-arms is slightly taller and a lot stockier short black hair covers his head, his face clean-shaven, and his eyes green.

"Torran" The scout turns back to the throne at Byrads voice, "I am going to the north to explain to the people what is going on. I will need you to come with me."

Torran pales but nods. Byrad turns to his guards and introduces them, "Kirin Forl" Mutton chops nods, "Arnic Carn." The stocky one nods as well. Byrad continues, "We four are going to help the king of Erandor and hopefully stop Tammaras army. I know that is a lot to accomplish but it is what we must attempt." The doors open and the smith master enters, his apprentices carrying three large chests.

Byrad stands and motions for the others to follow, "The Smith has created new armour for you."

The smith opens the first chest and hands out full suits of plate-mail. The armour is very thin and light made from some type of white metal, barely thicker than leather. The chain mail at the joints and neck is finely woven and as flexible as cloth.

Kirin laughs, "You're joking, this stuff couldn't stop a dagger."

The smith turns to him. "Put it on." he says in his soft deep voice, Kirin glances at Byrad, who smirks and nods.

Kirin dons the armour, marvelling at the lightness, looking up he sees the smith turn back to him with a huge battle-axe in hand. Before the guard can do anything he is on his back, looking down he sees the armour is undamaged, the axe head is dulled. Standing with some help from Torran the guard stares at the smith, "Thanks for the demonstration."

The others don the armour and the smith hands out open helms with nose guards, and oval shields that have the longest points at elbow and hand made from the same metal.

"This armour is the very strongest I am able to forge. It is light and tough only the very strongest beings could dent it, and as you saw a bladed weapon is almost useless after one hit." No one misses the use of the word 'beings' and each feel slightly less safe in the new armour.

Ammaris steps forward,

"Each of you are going to need something extra, something to give you an advantage and allow you to fight and kill the soldiers of Tammara." The sorcerer looks at each of the men and they can see in his eyes the pending sacrifice he is to make, "Byrad has his sword and shield, they are both powerfully enchanted with sorcery, I will similarly enchant a weapon of yours, make it a Rune-sword. They will be less potent but still give you an edge in a battle with chaos' new forces."

Byrad speaks up as Ammaris steps back,

"You all know what we face get some rest, tomorrow Ammaris will begin. We leave in five days, any questions?"

Arnic raises his hand, "Why not give us weapons made from that metal, wouldn't that give us an advantage?"

Byrad looks to the smith, who nods,

"Agreed you would assume so, but the metal will not hold an edge, something in the mix prevents it."

The group nod and after a moment and no more questions they all leave the room. Byrad stays were he is and watches Ammaris exit, his friend was undertaking a lot and the lord of Branight could think of no way to help. But with a sudden inspiration he realises could help his friend in another way. Calling for a clerk and sets about issuing a new law and decree.

Ammaris lays the last broadsword within the enchanting circle. The sorcerer had enchanted the other two over the last two days, he had sacrificed his power for Byrad, the city and the rest of the lands. He kneels next to the sword and begins to cast the enchantment,

"CORRELIA, HYLNOR~SITAST, CILNATI"

The magic, the power, the *life* is ripped from Ammaris and he cries out and collapses in the circle. A low moan escapes his lips and he feels his very soul is a lesser force than it was. The act of enchanting means that a physical change has occurred in the world and the target, the items, are now permanently enchanted, but in order for this change to happen there must be a power behind it that power is the sorcerers power, his soul. Ammaris could feel his loss.

Of course that loss means that he has lost the *power* to cast spells, all he has now are the few powerful artefacts left by the sorcerers. He could barely cast a light any more, "My sacrifice to you Byrad." he mutters bitterly then the sorcerers eyes move to the open book on the desk, a book he had found in a secret room of his new study. The old study of Amryd. It told him of very important things, knowledge that had been lost for millennia, knowledge the gods and two particular gods would not wish to be known. The sorcerer grins as he picks up his staff, his new staff. It feels warm to his touch but the sorcerer knew that was just an illusion, a figment of his imagination. But though there was no heat, no warmth he could still feel the magic he had cast into it, a magic that would give him the power to regain that which he had lost, for the book had given him insight into the *power* of the gods themselves.

Ammaris grins, how ironic it was that the very power to destroy the gods had been within a sorcerers' power ever since Karmarthen, and possibly before him, if the hints in the book were true. Ammaris made a mental note to research that.

Ammaris picks up the sword, Torrans, and walks to a table and places the weapon with the others. Then the sorcerer wearily walks to his bedchamber, the staff aids his steps and he crawls into bed.

Ammaris cradles his staff as he drifts off to sleep.

The group stand in the courtyard of Byrads palace, Torran, Arnic and Kirin each wear the new armour but each also has an empty scabbard. Ammaris had sent word he would meet them before they left for the north and return the weapons. Byrad checks the horses for the tenth time and wanders back to the other three.

"My lord," Says Kirin "do you think he is coming?"

Byrad nods, "If Ammaris says he'll meet us he will."

The group turn as a door opens and Ammaris steps out, dressed in a dark cloak, green robes a satchel pack and a new staff of pine. The sorcerer hurries over to the group handing out the weapons.

"Amm are you coming with us?"

"No but I will travel with you to the northern border. Guards," Ammaris turns to the three men and gets their attention, "These weapons are potent but my

power is limited, when either of you fight a Chaos-creature fight together." Ammaris then walks to a horse he had had brought from the stables. Mounting it he turns back, "Come on then, we should be going."
 The others quickly mount up and they ride out the north gates.
They travel north and over the bridge of Branight, Ammaris pulls up and stops,
"I leave here Byrad." The sorcerer points east along an old trail.
"Oh." Byrad looks east, "what's there?"
The sorcerer smiles lopsidedly, "Hopefully something I need." He says.
Byrad raises his eyebrows but the sorcerer looks away, obviously not going to answer.
"Thank you," says Torran fingering the sword on his back. The others add their thanks and Ammaris hesitantly shakes their hands. Then with a final wave he gallops his horse eastwards.
Byrad watches his friend go then turns northwards, the four men head into the grasslands.

As the group of horsemen travel on, Torran watches with some amusement as Arnic and Kirin try to adjust the swords at their hips, "What's the matter?"
Arnic turns at the scout's question, "These bloody horses make carrying these swords a nightmare!"
Kirin agrees and they look at Byrad, he rides easily, the sword of Branight at his side,
"How does he do it?" asks Kirin softly.
Torran grins, "I don't know, but as a scout I have always worn the sword on my back, it is far easier to ride that way."
Kirin looks at him with scepticism, "What if we need to draw the weapon quickly?"
Torran shakes his head, "A scout is not supposed to get into a fight, if you do then you should be ready."
Arnic and Kirin look at each other and unbuckle their swords, and replace them on their backs. As the group travel onwards the plains stretch in all directions, they keep to what shelter they can find, shallow hills and small dips cover the edges of the grass lands. The group slow as the wind changes and the stench of death flows over them. Rounding a small hillock they

find themselves in tiny valley between hills, ahead of them are bodies.

Nomadic warriors lie strewn about, broken and twisted something powerful had destroyed them, something capable of slashing through leather armour, flesh and bone. Nearby is a twisted corpse wearing robes of pale blue now stained in blood. Byrad glances at his naked blade, it was dull, and the Lord of Branight dismounts, he turns the body over and bows his head,

"May Élan-vital keep you safe, Brother Hin-lak."

The priest was clutching the remains of a battle-axe, its haft blackened the head a solid pool of metal. After Byrad has prayed for the souls of the fallen he remounts and the group rides north. No explanation was needed for the dead nomads it was clear Tammara was responsible, she had left the city of Branight and headed north through the nomads land.

At dusk the foursome make camp and in the gloom of night they eat a cold meal and sleep as well as they can. Byrad takes first watch and sits listening to the sounds of the nocturnal plains, a wolf howls in the distance. Byrad sits still and listens, he frowns as he realises he can hear nothing except the breathing of his companions, a silence leaden with foreboding settles over the grasslands and the camp. Standing he draws his sword and it flares into light,

"BEWARE!" Byrads shout echoes over the campsite.

Instantly awake the two guards and the scout look around. Within the circle of Byrads flaring light, the companions see four cloaked beings.

As they see them the companions from Branight feel fear eat into their minds and souls, with hideous screams the beings shed their cloaks revealing horror.

Byrad, Torran, Arnic and Kirin step back from the chaos that stands before them, the beings had once been human, but this was only a vague assumption. They were man shaped two arms two legs a head, but they were mutilated and defiled. Black ooze issues from open wounds all over their bodies and their bodies were covered in scabrous sores.

The friends look around at the creatures and find that in their fear and shock they were now surrounded. Byrad grips his sword tighter and launches himself at the beings he brings his sword to bare and the creature

145

backs away. The others step forward into battle and they are soon fighting furiously.

Torran swings his sword at the being before him, it blocks the blow and screams as the magic cuts into it then punches out and Torran is slammed to the ground. Kirin sees the scout fall and he slashes wildly at his opponent forcing it back, then the guard turns and shouts as he races towards the creature baring down on Torran,

"Arnic, come on!"

The other guardsman glances over and ducks an attack, with a cry he severs the clawed hand and runs after Kirin. They reach their fallen comrade and savagely attack the creature, it screams horribly and tries to defend itself. Torran scrambles to his feet, shaking, and joins the murderous melee. The creature falls under the heavy, enchanted broadswords and soon its screams cease. Torran continues to hack at the remains until Kirin grabs his shoulders and pulls him away.

The trio turn back to Byrad and see he had dispatched one, but now was hard pressed by the remaining creatures. They run in screaming and soon there are only four exhausted men and four stains. As the last one dies Byrads sword returns to its normal sheen and they endeavour to rebuild their fire.

"Those were some of the ones I saw at Tammaras camp." Says Torran quietly as they sit huddled around the fire, "they were obviously responsible for the nomads."

Byrad nods and looks at the three, "You all fought well."

Arnic frowns, "We should have listened to the sorcerer though, you alone are able to kill those things." He wipes his damp forehead, "We have to fight together."

The group falls silent again, then after a moment Byrad speaks,

"We still have a long way to go, two weeks until we reach the northern kingdoms South Pass. Hopefully we will reach it with no more trouble."

The others look up and they all think the same, they settle back to rest but none are able to sleep well.

The companions travel northward, they find shelter where they can and stay with nomadic tribes that have heard of Byrad and his teachings. The four men travel on always alert even though they had not seen any other of Tammaras army since that one night. They make good time and soon come to a trading post, about three days from the South pass of the Northern Kingdom.

They step through the gates warily and quickly make their way to a small inn. The stress of the last week and a half makes the companions edgy; and as they wait for the innkeeper their hands hover near weapons, and they watch the others in the common room suspiciously.

"Yes, how can I help?" the innkeeper steps back at the sudden stares he receives, he glances at Byrads sword, half out of its scabbard. Byrads gaze comes up from the dull metal blade and he meets the innkeepers look.

"A room for four, please" He states, looking quickly over to the door as another customer enters. The innkeeper nods and quickly hands over a key.

"It is the second door on the left." He points down a hallway to the left of the bar. "Sirs," He adds softly, "You need not fear anything here. I post guards each night." The companions pause and nod slightly.

The room was large and had four beds, soft mattresses show the inns wealth and the companions sit in exhausted silence. Suddenly the door opens and the innkeeper steps into the room, he stops when he sees four swords drawn and pointing his way.

"Sorry sirs." He says trying to keep his voice steady, "but I can have water heated for baths, if you wish."

The companions sheath their weapons and Byrad nods, "Yes please. And if you could knock before you enter." The innkeeper nods and apologises again as he leaves. Torran crosses to the door and holds a hand out to Byrad, the noble man and priest throws the key over to him and the scout locks the door. The men struggle out of their armour and lie back on their beds.

The companions are awoken to a knock on the door, Byrad calls out as he draws his sword, it stays dull, "Who is it?"

"Sir, the water is ready."

Byrad relaxes and he unlocks the door, the innkeeper is waiting for them and leads them down the hall. The wash room is a large expensive room with ten sunken baths, four of which steam, a fire warms the room from a large hearth on the left. Byrad thanks the innkeeper and locks the door as the man leaves.

The companions undress and slip into the baths, each has his sword naked and near by. Byrad touches the hilt of his now and again.

Byrad awakes to a soft knock on the door, he wakes his friends and they dry themselves with towels kept in stone shelves near the fire. Wrapping the towels around themselves and picking up their swords Byrad opens the door. The innkeeper is stood waiting,

"Sirs, would you like come to the common room for dinner?" Byrad looks to his friends and after a moment they nod. "Good." beams the innkeeper.

"Could you have our clothes cleaned?" asks Byrad. The innkeeper nods and the four men thank him and head back to their room. Changing into some clean clothes, the companions' belt on their swords and walk to the main room of the inn, the innkeeper sees them and motions to a table in the corner. Sitting down the friends' have a free view of the room and the exits leading from it including the stairs.

A serving girl walks over and asks for their order.

"Four ales please," Says Byrad, "What food do you have?"

"We have Beef stew, Beef served with potatoes and vegetables, Fresh bread, strong cheese and cold meats."

After a few moments the friends order four Beef and potato meals. The girl nods and walks over to the bar returning quickly with their drinks.

The following morning the companions leave the trading station and head north once again. They travel a well-laid road built as a fast route for traders and merchants from the Northern Kingdom to the trading station. Still the companions have three days of travel ahead of them.

As they finally reach the outskirts of the South Pass late on the third days travel the group see the stone walled town of Angar. Even as they watch the great oaken gates of the fortress town open, and a troop of soldiers ride out, lances raised.

They ride up to the companions and the captain salutes, "Good evening, sirs. What business do you have here?"

Byrad looks at the captain and the guardsmen, he leans forward and speaks to the captain noticing one old veteran looking at him strangely.

"We have travelled a long way and would like some rest."

The captain nods, but he also shakes his head, "I must ask you to explain your reason for travelling to our great kingdom."

Byrad stares at the man but he sees the captain would only let them pass if he was satisfied with their answers.

The noble man nods and sits back in the saddle, "Well captain, we understand you are under attack."

Byrads statement takes the guardsmen by surprise and they lower their lances, Byrad raises his hand and his companions pause in drawing their swords.

"How do you know this? We have kept it secret from everyone not of the kingdom."

"I am afraid my scouts have been to your front lines."

The captain stares at Byrad in shock, and then asks, "Who are you?"

"My name is Byrad Branight, I am the Lord of Bra..."

Byrads words trail off as the captains face pales, and the veteran guard nods to himself.

"My Lord," Says the captain struggling to regain his composure, "please follow us, we shall escort you to the town."

With that they head for the gates, the captain orders one of his men to ride in haste to the town and inform the duke of Byrads imminent arrival.

"Captain, you know my name?" asks Byrad.

"Yes sir. You are the descendent of Dynadryd Branight..." Byrad nods as the captain continues, "who defeated the Chaos-warriors and a great Dragon possessed of chaos."

It was Byrads turn to look surprised, "How do you know this?"

The captain looks at Byrad incredulously, "Everyone knows of that great time in history." The captain looks closer at Byrad, "Surely you know of it?" he asks.

Byrad nods, "Yes, but only recently. I knew of Dynadryds battle against the army of monsters, but not that he had journeyed north."

The captain shakes his head in disbelief, "We are taught of the Warmonger Dynadryd from our early schooling. The monks teach us all of the ancient history and the knowledge that we all need."

Byrad nods but does not speak, he could almost hear Ammaris, *'the religions teach only what they want you to know.'* Could his friend have been right, it seemed like his entire schooling was a lie, and he already knew that the priests had lied... had exaggerated about the sorcerers' actions and motivations, even if they, being priests of Laumas-Nahtan, had not resorted to the executions.

The captain sees that Byrad is lost in thought and leaves him be. They travel up to the gates of the town in silence but as they ride in he turns to Byrad,

"My Lord Branight, welcome to Angar, and the Kingdom of Erandor!"

Byrad looks up and sees a very well kept town, clean stone paths run on either side of the road they ride on, and the road is paved with large slabs of stone. The buildings are white washed, the people that look on the impromptu parade are seemingly well fed and healthy. Byrads sees that most of the populace seem to be soldiers, if very young.

"The Lord Byrad Branight, descendent of the Great Dynadryd Branight comes to our town of Angar!" The captain shouts out the announcement and after a shocked silence the people of Angar begin to cheer.

Byrad, Arnic, Kirin and Torran look around in pleased wonder. Byrad looks at the captain and he just shrugs, "You *are* descended from a hero."

The group ride up to a large building, obviously the home of the Duke of Angar. The said Duke is speaking with the guard that had been sent ahead. As the group ride up, a growing crowd behind them, the Lord turns away from the man and strides over to the dismounting captain.

"Captain!" he snaps, "What is going on? I have one of you men telling me that the Lord of Branight is coming, and now we have some sort of riot!"

The captain looks embarrassed and he steps over to the lord and speaks with him discreetly. Byrad dismounts and stands next to his horse and studies the Lord of Angar.

He is tall and thin, dressed in trousers that are baggy around the knees and bright scarlet red. His shirt is made from some shiny cloth and is bright green, at the

Lords hip is a long delicate rapier. Byrad shakes his head in disgust, another pampered and pompous lord too full of his own import to lead properly.

The Duke of Angar strides arrogantly over to Byrad, leaving the captain mid way through speaking. The aristocrat looks at Byrad up and down, noting with obvious disgust the dust that covers him and the armour and weapons he wears.

"So you *claim* to be a Branight, descended from Dynadryd himself?" the Duke of Angar scoffs.

Byrad stares at the man, "The name of my ancestor is Dynadryd. And I am a Branight." Byrad speaks softly but firmly.

"Oh come on now lad, Stop this charade!" The lord laughs, "Tell the truth."

Byrads eyes narrow and his brows nit over his nose, he steps forward and though the lord of Angar is taller than Byrad he stumbles backwards and sprawls on the ground.

"Truth!" asks Byrad through gritted teeth, "*You* want to know the truth." Byrad steps forward again and leans on one knee, leaning over the terrified lord of Angar. "The truth is you are a fool, unworthy of your title and position. I've met bandits that were nobler than you I come here to help you defeat an army." Byrad leans forward and growls his next words, "My people were turned to undead, my father was the vampire lord over them and he was the servant of the last Chaos-Warrior."

The people gasp at that, and the lord trembles. Byrad steps away, but still angry he drags free his sword and points it at the lord, "This is my blade. The sword of Branight to use against the Chaos-Warriors that are the army you fight, I bring this to you." He lifts his eyes to the crowd and they look at him silently. Byrad stands there a moment then sheaths the sword and leads his horse to an inn.

Torran, and the two guards step into the inn and see Byrad stood at the bar draining a mug of ale. They look at each other and step over to their Lord.

"Byrad, you all right?" asks Kirin.

"Aaahhh," Byrad puts the empty mug on the bar, "I'm fine." He sees Kirin's expression and laughs; "Seriously I'm ok."

The innkeeper comes over,

"Sir, is there anything else?"

"Yes, we need four rooms, baths, food and more ale!" Byrad nods to a table in the corner and after getting more ale they walk over and sit.

Some hours later the two guards and Byrad return to their table after bathing. Torran indicating his tiredness had gone to his room. Ordering ale Byrad and Arnic drink half of theirs in one swallow and Kirin just shakes his head.

"Come on!" says Arnic, "Drink it, don't just sip it."

As they laugh Kirin turns to Byrad, but the priest's attention seems elsewhere. Following his gaze Kirin sees a red haired barmaid walking towards their table, the two guards look at each other and roll their eyes.

The barmaid expertly delivers their meals and Byrad smiles as he thanks her.

Byrad wakes early the next morning, a loss of feeling in his left arm. He turns his head and looks at the sleeping form of the barmaid, her name was Suzan he recalls. For a while he just lies there thinking and watching her sleep. Eventually he eases his arm from under her and climbs out of bed and dresses, quietly he opens the door and walks down stairs.

Byrad walks out into the town and even though it wasn't official (that Byrad was the descendant of Dynadryd) the few people he met bowed or curtsied. Byrad in turn waved and greeted those he saw.

The captain was one such he met.

"Good morning, Captain." Says Byrad as the man comes up to him, Byrad stops at a flower seller and studies different roses.

"My Lord," says the man bowing, "my name is Zanric."

Byrad nods and glances at Zanric, "And my name is Byrad."

"Byrad, I bring apologies from my Lord of Angar. He regrets that he upset and offended you."

Byrad stares at Zanric for a moment then looks back at the roses. Picking one dark red he dips a hand into his pouch.

"The Duke sent you to apologise." Byrad murmurs as he fishes out some coins, "Tell him if he wants to apologise he will find me at the Inn." Byrad hands the flower seller the money easily four times what was needed.

"I thought you might say that." Zanric sighs, then changing the subject he asks, "Byrad what are your plans?"

Byrad nods to the woman he had just paid and walks back to wards the inn, "I'm not entirely sure. I need to know the situation better. If you set up a meeting with the Duke for midday I will figure something out, insure you're there too." With that Byrad walks into the inn.

Byrad steps out onto the street and heads for the Lords palace, it was still early morning but he wanted to see the duke alone. He quickly reaches the gates and the guards on duty come to attention. As he strides through an aide to the Lord appears at the main entrance, bowing to Byrad.

"My Lord Byrad, please follow me the Duke awaits you in his study."

Byrad is led through the opulent palace of the Duke of Angar, at home Byrads own palace was different. It had none of the finery of this place, and his was a palace for worship to the Life god and as a place for pure ruler ship of the city.

As he is led to the study Byrad shakes his head and wonders what the Duke will say when he hears his plans. The aide stops at the door and opening it announces Byrad.

"Lord Byrad Branight!"

Byrad walks into the study and sees a sight that makes him consider reassessing the Duke. The man, dressed in simple but expensive black tunic and trousers sits at a desk over flowing with papers. He looks up and smiles.

"Lord Byrad, please come in." He gestures to a chair and glancing once at his desk walks over and extends his hand.

Byrad shakes the proffered hand and looks into the dukes face, "You look tired Duke..."

The man nods, "Gallant, my name is Gallant. And yes I am tired." He walks back to his desk and sits heavily.

Byrad looks at the man and sits opposite him.

Duke Gallant looks up and sees Byrads gaze, he smiles.

"I don't look like the same pompous popinjay you met the other day, do I?"

Byrad smiles slightly, "No you don't."

The Duke leans back and motions to the paper work on his desk, "These are the reports from the front lines. The King has ordered me to send more troops."

Byrad frowns slightly and the Duke sits forward, "This town is the training area for the new recruits, the King wants me to send all those who are ready or had the minimum three months training."

Byrad shakes his head, "It won't be enough."

"I know!" snaps the Duke then he puts his head in his hands, "Sorry. Its just I don't know what I can do."

Byrad sits silent for a moment and sees the Duke of Angar in a new light, but he also realises the man was close to falling apart. He leans forward and grips his shoulder, "Let me help, Gallant."

The Duke looks up and a weight seems to lift a little. "Thank you, Byrad."

For the next hour the two men sort through the reports and requisitions. Byrad sees that the Duke is a very good ruler, he had made the training of the recruits the highest priority and his decisions were thought out long and hard. Byrad finds himself respecting the Duke of Angar and his efforts to keep the town running.

Just as the town bells chime the midday hour the two men finish the last report. The door opens and Zanric is announced, as are Byrads companions. The captain of the town guard walks in and takes in the sight of the two lords, he steps up to the desk and salutes the Duke.

"My Lord this report just came."

Gallant takes the sealed letter and opens it, as Byrad and Zanric watch the Duke of Angar pales and his hands shake as he drops the letter, "I should have sent the men." He says softly lowering his head into his hands. Byrad scoops up the letter and reads aloud,

"The King has fallen and his son holds the Border-wall. Refugees from the Kings City of Erandor, and the Princes City of Greystone along with all towns and villages are ordered to Angar.' Then he hands it to Zanric.

"Gallant," says Byrad, "If those recruits had been sent, it would have made no difference."

The Duke looks up and nods as he tries to compose himself, "What should we do?"

Byrad nods and takes a breath as he stands, "Gallant you know the army you fight is now headed by Chaos." The Duke nods, and Byrad continues, "The soldiers your people are fighting are now Chaos-Warriors, they can not be killed by sword and arrow alone." Byrad turns to his scouts, "We four have weapons of sorcery enchantment, and they will kill Chaos."

Gallant sits back as Byrad finishes, his sharp mind already figuring some thing out,

"Byrad why are you here?" He asks.

Byrad nods and looks grim, "Obviously you realise that it was in recent months that Chaos was involved in the army that attacks you. That is because Chaos was once my companion."

Byrad begins to explain the last half-year of his life, and the meeting of Tammara. When he finishes the Duke shakes his head in disbelief.

"So it is down to you." Gallant sighs and looks at Byrad, "Our duty as rulers is a difficult one isn't it." Gallant stands and looks at those from Branight, "You four cannot defeat an army." He states, "What is your plan."

Byrad nods, "I alone have a sword powerful enough to kill the Chaos-Warriors out right, these others need to be used in conjunction, but I think we can get more weapons."

Gallant frowns, "We have no such weapons and as far as I am aware we have no Sorcerers."

"You know of the tomb of my ancestor though."

The Duke nods still frowning until he smiles suddenly, "The Hundred Warriors of Dynadryd!" he exclaims.

Byrad nods, "Exactly. There are a hundred Rune-swords, we will have to retrieve them."

The Duke begins to pace, he calls out and the aide quickly enters the room, the Duke orders provisions prepared for a troop to be sent to the mountain tomb of Dynadryd Branight. As the aide rushes off Gallant turns to the captain and orders him prepare a troop.

"Captain," he calls stopping the man at the door, "Take some of the veterans away from training along with the best trainees." Zanric nods and leaves.

Chapter Eighteen

Byrad watches the stablemen prepare in the courtyard. He can see the pure military precision that Gallant obviously insists on, and even though the troop consists mainly of trainees they all know what they do, their lances held rock solid. Byrad takes a second look and it occurs to him that there is an air of grimness that would only ever be associated with veterans. These boys he realises are soldiers by choice as well as necessity. They know that if they do not do well and if they do not train hard they will have no kingdom left.

Byrad turns to the duke and staggers, he falls to his knees and grips his head.

*

Byrad awakens on a shadowy plane, he knows he is not alone and turns. With bowed head he meets his God.

"Lord Élan Vital, have I died?" he asks, still aware of throbbing pain in his temple.

The God of life shakes his head, "No, you yet live. I have information for you, and I needed to tell you in person."

"Brother, hurry I can not hold his essence indefinitely." The whispered words come from Byrads left and he turns seeing the god Ackza.

Élan Vital nods to his brother, "Yes. Byrad we have found out that Tammara has sent minions to ambush any who attempt to take the swords you seek."

Byrad nearly curses as he hears the words and he thinks he almost sees his God smile,

"How did she know?"

"*Brother!*"

Élan Vital turns to his brother and nods almost impatiently, "You must go now Byrad or you may well die. She might be Chaos-mad but she is not stupid, she knows that sorcery is the only thing that can stop her."

As the words are spoken the plane rocks and the two gods stagger, then Byrads pain is gone and he blinks.

*

"Byrad are you ok?" Duke Gallant leans over the blinking prostrate form of Byrad. The priest and noble man sits up and accepts Gallants helping hand.

"I'm fine." He looks out the window and sees the troop prepare to leave. "Stop them!" he says to the Duke.

Gallant stares at Byrad a moment, but he steps out onto his balcony and shouts down to Zanric.

"Hold, Captain!"

With sharp commands the troop are halted and the two Lords hurry down to the courtyard.

"What is it Byrad?"

Byrad looks to Gallant and explains, "I am High priest to the god Élan Vital, he spoke to me. He has revealed that Tammara has set a trap for any who try to retrieve the swords."

Gallant stops and stares at Byrad strangely, Byrad looks round and stops also, "What?"

Gallant looks at Byrad and steps closer, "You worship a God?" Gallants tone is hard to place.

The Duke seems to be trying to keep it neutral, but Byrad detects something of Ammaris in the way the words are said.

"Yes."

Gallant takes Byrads arm and leads him into a small room, he looks at the maid and she hurries out.

"Byrad, we worship no gods in this Kingdom. And if you want to keep the respect of my people you would do well to keep your beliefs to your self."

Byrad stands in shocked silence and he sits down on a nearby stool. Again he hears Ammaris' voice, or is it his own.

Then some thing he had heard Zanric say clicked into place, looking at Gallant he asks, "Your people are taught by the Monks of Knowledge?"

"Yes, they teach us, and when I say *us* I mean all of our citizens rich or poor not just those who worship."

Byrad nods and stands, "Gallant..." The Duke also stands almost at attention, stiff, rigid and cold

"Gallant I am still Byrad." Byrad says softly.

Gallant lets out a breath and smiles slightly, "Yes, of course. Sorry Byrad it's just no one..." he trails off.

Byrad nods, "I understand." He says the words and he suddenly understands some of what Ammaris', what a *sorcerers'* life must have been like. Some thing else

157

occurs to him, "You do know you are at war against a God?"

"Yes, the monks have taught us all about Chaos and its manifestations. But my people have been committed to the destruction of Chaos for centuries." Gallant realises that Byrad has no such knowledge, "Byrad we will speak at length about this, there is much you should know, but we must sort out this problem first."

The two men walk quickly to the courtyard where confused stablemen prepare horses. They snap to attention when the two Lords step out.

"Captain, walk with us we have a problem."

The three men head towards the barracks and the training grounds beyond. As they turn the corner they see Torran, Arnic and Kirin training three different groups.

Zanric stops as he is told the news, "How did she find out?" he asks shocked.

The two Lords glance at each other then Gallant says, "She is a God, Zanric."

The captain nods and looks a little lost, he asks, "What now?"

Gallant turns to Byrad and sees him deep in thought as he watches the training.

"What is it?"

Byrad looks at Gallant with a slight smile, "I have an idea. Each of your troops consists of twenty-five men and a lieutenant. We will train these soldiers to use the weapons of the hundred. We will have them led by me and my scouts, we will go to the front lines and help in the defence."

Gallant nods, "Not a bad plan. But what about *getting* the swords?"

Byrad grins, "If Zanric doesn't mind I will go with them."

Zanric looks up and shakes his head, "No I don't mind." He chuckles a little nervously.

Byrad looks over to the three scouts, "*They* will be a problem." He says softly.

"That is out of the question, my Lord!" Arnic and Kirin say together, they sit with the Duke and Byrad in the study.

"If you go, we go." Adds Kirin, "You can not know what Tammara has sent to protect the tomb."

Byrad sighs but when Torran leans forward he looks up into his pale face, "They are right, Byrad." He states, "You will die if you go alone," He stands and walks over to a table and a jug of ale and some mugs "we will probably die even if we go together." He mutters as he drains the ale and pours some more into his mug.

Silence settles on the room and Kirin looks at Byrad, "We go together." He says, and Byrad realises they would.

Gallant clears his throat, "So tomorrow you leave." He says.

Byrad nods and stands, he looks over at Torran who is staring out the window refilling his mug. Arnic rises and shakes his head as Byrad is about to speak. Byrad nods and they leave the room, The Duke shuts the door leaving Torran alone in the study.

The four troops mount up as Byrad and Gallant step out into the courtyard. Gallant had decided to send all four troops for the mission was dangerous and imperative. Byrad mounts up and the Duke stands before them all.

"Men," He says looking at the hundred that were mounted on restless horses, they looked nervous "You are going on a dangerous mission but I know you are capable of completing it, though you may feel unprepared you have trained hard and now you will fight for your Kingdom. These four are your lieutenants and Captain Zanric will be with you also. Bring us back the means of our salvation." With that he salutes.

The troops turn and move through the town and out of the gates, the people watch and cheer as they ride past.

Byrad naturally leads and they head east following the mountains beginning the four day ride. After some time scouts are sent ahead from each troop, they are ordered to observe only and if anything, even tracks are found, then they should return at once. The troop travel tense and alert for not only were they entering a trap set by Tammara, they were also entering an area inhabited by monsters of a more mundane sort.

When they make camp the lieutenants eat with their men, making sure the soldiers were well and moral high. Just as the troops pack away the hasty camp three scouts ride in and go straight to the Captain.

Byrad and the others move over and the captain relays their reports.

"About two miles ahead of us are tracks of something large, none of the men could identify them. Also a large group of Orcs are camped about two hours ride from here."

Byrad nods, "How many Orcs?"

Zanric looks grim "Approximately a hundred and fifty."

"Can we evade them?"

The Captain shakes his head, "No, they are right next to the route we are taking."

"Damn. Prepare the men, tell them to ready weapons and be ready for a fight."

The troops soon ride on and some two hours later they see the Orcs. The creatures are now spread over the path, seeing the humans they snarl in anger and hatred. Byrad pulls free his sword and with a shout he rides forward, his twenty-five close behind lances lowered. The rest of the troops gallop in and soon the mountains echo with the sound battle, screams of the dying fill the air and blood stains the ground.

The troops gallop through the Orcs and reform at the opposite end.

"How did we do, Captain." asks Byrad.

The Captain turns and after a moment he answers, "We have four wounded but no fatalities."

Byrad smiles and shouts, "Well done lads! Let's see if we can sort these curs out!"

A great cheer rises and the troops prepare to charge again, those without lances now draw broad swords and prepare to attack. As the soldiers ride forward the Orcs turn and flee into the mountains. The soldiers rein in their horses and watch in surprise, as over a hundred Orcs flee from them. The soldiers begin to rejoice but then one terrified scream cuts through the mountains.

Byrad turns and sees Torran staring up the path, then the creatures bound into view and Byrad shouts to the troops, "All of you stay back you can not fight these things, when you have a chance race to the tomb!"

With that Byrad, Arnic and Kirin race to Torrans side, the scout shakes with fear, but as the creatures close in on them he shivers once then sits still and pale.

The creatures, like the ones from Branight bound towards the three humans and the men see there are five of the monstrosities.

Byrad shouts his battle cry and his sword blazes with whiteness, then they race in. The creatures stumble back for they were used to their pray running. Byrads sword slashes into one creature and it screams out its death. Torran, Arnic and Kirin also battle frantically but it was obvious the other creatures would be on them in moments. Arnic blocks a blow but receives another to his chest he falls from his horse and the creature bears down on him.

Arnic looks up from his dented breastplate and sees his death, but the creature above him screams as it is thrust aside. Arnic scrambles to his feet and sees the troops had charged the creatures as the dust clears he sees the creatures are dead or dying, lances still embedded in them.

Byrad and the other lieutenants quickly end the lives of the struggling creatures and silence returns to the mountains.

"I thought it was only sorcery that could injure these things." says Zanric breathing hard.

Byrad shrugs, "We thought it was. Any way I thought I told you to go to the tomb."

Zanric copies Byrads shrug and the lord grips his shoulder, "Report!" he calls.

They had lost twelve soldiers, a testament to their training, Arnic was fine if badly bruised and there were light wounds through out the troops.

After a while they mount up again and the soldiers travel on up the path. Scouts are sent out again and the group make their way to the tomb. They know that their fight is not over Tammara would have sent more than the five Beasts.

Early evening comes with the scouts returning with no news, a camp is made in a defensive potion on the trail, patrols are set up and the troops try and relax as they eat a cold meal. With nightfall the troops try to sleep, but though they were soldiers and had seen action, they were still only trainees. Byrad and others try to relax their men and eventually they do sleep, after a fashion.

Byrad, Zanric and the others move away from the sleeping men and speak in hushed voices,

"What do you think is waiting for us?" asks Zanric.

Byrad shakes his head and Torran answers, "That is the thing with chaos, it could be any thing. Those demons we've met before, but Tammara can corrupt any thing with her power."

Byrad nods and turns to Zanric, "I suggest we send a scouting party tomorrow morning before we set off again. We four," he indicates Arnic, Kirin and Torran. "Should go, if any thing happens we have weapons that will help. We should probably go in separate directions with maybe three others."

Zanric nods and they return to their bed rolls and try to sleep. Torran lies awake and shivers, he was terrified. There was no other term for it, he would scout and try and teach his men the best way to avoid the Chaos-beings, but could he be the leader Byrad wanted. Who ever heard about a terrified leader, frightened or afraid, but terrified? No it was a task for someone other than Torran.

The troops stand ready and waiting for their orders, Byrad steps forward,

"We need to know what Chaos has set up for us. We need three sets of volunteers for scouting parties."

Nearly ninety hands rise at the request, Byrad shakes his head and turns to Zanric.

"You know their strengths and weaknesses pick the best."

Zanric nods and walks among the troops. He looks for the most talented veterans but soon realises that, though they maybe veterans they did not have the skills for a scout mission. He would need young eyes and ears, quick reactions and pure discipline, quantities in good supply but they also needed courage and fear, for fear keeps a man alert and alive and not many men would admit or accept being afraid.

Zanric stops by one group, he looks at the men and sees one or two down turned heads. He smiles slightly and picks two others then stands near the other two, their heads raise and he looks at them a moment,

"Soldiers!" He snaps, instantly the men are standing rigid, "How do you feel?" Asks the captain the men frown and hesitate, their eyes flicker to their colleagues then to the Captain.

The group quieten and Zanric simply watches the two men, then they answer almost in unison,

"Scared sir, I will not put myself forward."

Zanric nods and he notes some mutterings from the other troops, he walks to the two men and puts a hand on each shoulder,

"Well said men, but you *will* be coming." He turns to the other troopers and they snap to attention, "Men the things we are up against deserve our fear, as much as they deserve our hate. These two will come because they see that respect is due Chaos."

Zanric leads the four men away and he begins to choose again.

The four groups under the command of Byrad, Kirin, Arnic and Torran head forwards into the territory surrounding the tomb of Dynadryd and the Hundred. They all manage to make their way to the cliffs surrounding the entrance to the tomb, what they see makes them worried. Nothing.

Not one Chaos-warrior stands below, though when Byrad draws his sword it flares with a warning glare.

The group work their way back and Byrads sword dims, its warning glow extinguishes.

*

Zanric stares at Byrad as he listens to the report,

"What do you mean: 'Nothing there'?" He asks.

"Exactly that, we saw nothing but my sword glowed in warning. So something was there."

Zanric shakes his head, "Are you saying they are invisible?" he almost scoffs at the notion.

Torran frowns, "Remember Captain, Chaos is by definition random, it is totally unpredictable. Anything is possible."

Zanric looks at Torran and nods at the quietly spoken statement, "Fine, what can we do? If something is waiting at the tomb but we can't see it..."

Byrad shakes his head and an air of despondency settles over them, spreading quickly through the camp. That night, no solutions had been discovered and Byrad now kept his sword in hand. The troopers saw

163

this and fear began to set into their souls. Byrad shakes his head and steps into his tent.

"Hello Byrad."

Byrad swings round his sword extended as he hears the voice. His eyes see the robed intruder and he tries to stop the blow from severing Ammaris' head.

As the blade gets within half a meter of Ammaris it slams against solid nothingness, throwing Ammaris to the ground. Byrad drops the sword and rushes to his friend's side.

"Amm are you alright?" He asks in a shaking voice.

The sorcerer stands while Byrads helping hand stops at the edge of his protection, "*Oh yes I'm fine.*" He mutters but the smile takes away the sarcasm, "But I'd be happy with a handshake next time!" The sorcerer releases the magic with a quiet word.

Byrad grabs his friend in a hug then pushes him back, as he suddenly feels something odd. Looking at Ammaris Byrad sees an indescribable change.

"Amm you seem... different."

Ammaris smiles at that and sits on a camp chair, resting his staff against his shoulder, "What you can see or *feel*, to be precise, is my aura. I have my *power* back Byrad."

The priest looks at Ammaris and he could almost see the power held within him, far more power than the sorcerer had had before, even when they had first met. Byrad is about to ask something, but he suddenly gets the feeling he doesn't wish to know where his friend had got the power.

Ammaris looks at Byrad, "I understand you have a problem with Tammara."

"How did you know?"

"I have my ways." The sorcerer says grinning. "I will deal with the ambush." He reaches into his pack and pulls out a bedroll.

Byrad nods and picking up his sword walks to his bed removing his armour, "I'm glad you are here, we may have had to give up on this plan, and no simple swordsman could fight the invisible."

Ammaris freezes, as he is about to lay down, "What?"

Byrad turns at his friends question, "The ambush is with invisible Chaos warriors." He looks at Ammaris, "You didn't know, did you?"

The sorcerer shakes his head, "No. I must see the ambush site."

Byrad nods and is shocked by Ammaris' change of mood, just a moment a go he was confident, *powerful*, now he was very uneasy almost scared.

"We'll go tomorrow."

Ammaris hesitates then glancing at the darkening sky outside the tent, he nods.

The friends lay down for the night to sleep. Ammaris lies awake for a while his thoughts in turmoil, *invisible* chaos he had never heard of such a thing. His first thought was a horrible one, but if it proved true...

The sorcerer shivers and rolls over trying to forget his thoughts.

Morning comes with low clouds and threat of rain, the night had been quiet except for various bands of monsters: Trolls, Orcs and even Wyrms. All of these stayed clear of the human camp, they were intent on escaping the mountains.

Byrad, Ammaris and the others from Branight creep back to the vantage point. Byrad draws his sword and it shines, but below them is nothing. The priest turns to Ammaris and sees him going into a trance, suddenly the sorcerer jerks and stumbles away. He collapses against a rock pale and shaking.

"Amm, what is it?" Asks Byrad

The sorcerer shakes his head and tries to collect himself, he stands and looks down on the entrance to the tomb. Raising his hand he points down and begins to cast a spell, he smiles slightly and then suddenly the entrance way is revealed, as if it had always been and they just hadn't noticed.

The men gasp as they behold the threat that awaits them: a Dragon. Byrad and Ammaris recognise it as the same creature that they had come up against before. It was the same one that Dynadryd had defeated, though it cost him his life.

Byrad turns to Ammaris,

"Will you help us destroy that thing?"

The sorcerer looks at his friend for a moment in incredulous shock,

"Of course I will. Did you think I would just leave you all to die?"

Byrad shakes his head,

"Not at all," He says, "we would not necessarily all die."

"Are you mad?" Asks Ammaris, "That Dragon would rip your army to shreds, add the chaos which pervades it and you would not stand a chance. With me you will stand a chance." Ammaris pauses then adds, "Though it will be difficult even with my help."

The sorcerer walks back to camp and enters Byrads tent.

Byrad follows his friend, a troubled expression on his face, Ammaris was showing signs of arrogance and that was not a good or godly thing. Of course Ammaris was not religious but perhaps one day he would see the truth and join Élan-vital.

"Ammaris, what are we going to do?" Byrad asks as he enters the tent.

Ammaris looks up from his prone position on Byrads bed,

"Let me think on it, right now I need some rest." Ammaris rolls onto his side and calls out to Byrad just as he leaves, "Get together all the arrows your men have, and a barrel of water, no make it oil. Wake me in six hours."

Ammaris emerges from the tent and heads over to a barrel of drinking water. Taking a cup from a near by table he wanders over to Byrad and his Eighty-eight.

The sorcerer looks about and notices the men do not look away from him, nor do they sneer in hatred. Good of Byrad to order his men to behave, also he notes the arrows and barrel of oil.

"Ammaris, what will oil do for us. We won't hurt a Dragon with fire."

The sorcerer doesn't even look at his friend, instead he hands him his empty cup and walks to the barrel. Dipping his hands into the oil, he begins to murmur words of sorcery, as he withdraws his fingers the oil crackles with magic.

Ammaris turns to the soldiers and he sees the fake respect in their eyes,

"The enchantment I have placed on the oil will last for one hour only, you will wait for my signal and then attack."

Ammaris turns away then stops when a soldier hands him a towel. He takes it and begins walking away when he hears the soldier mutter something.

"What was that?"

The soldier looks rather annoyed, "Well *sir*, is it only you or all sorcerers that have no manners?"

Ammaris' eye brows rise in shock, "Why should I waste manners on people who only tolerate me?" Ammaris throws the oiled rag away.

"Sir what do you mean?"

"Byrad ordered you all to treat me with respect, you don't *really* respect me."

The soldier looks shocked now, "Sir, Lord Byrad has not made any orders regarding you. Why would we not respect you?"

"I am a *Sorcerer*."

The soldier shrugs, "So. We are grateful for your assistance, we have only ever had legends regarding Sorcerers, to meet one and see his magic... "

Ammaris stares at the soldier, "Don't your Priests teach you of our evil ways?"

The soldier stiffens, "Sir we have no priests, religion is outlawed in The Kingdom."

Ammaris nods, to say he was shocked was an understatement but he was also slightly amused. Byrad was now in a land that obviously despised religion, it was like a reverse of the Four Kingdoms, a thought occurs to Ammaris,

"Soldier, who is it that teaches in your land?"

"It is the monastic order of knowledge, sir."

Ammaris nods and smiles and bows slightly, "Thank you... "

"Private Arlter Mathius." The soldier salutes and runs back to the others.

Ammaris walks away, he scrambles down the rocks to the path that leads down to the tomb his mind spins with thoughts. This Kingdom would be perfect for a reestablishment of sorcery, to allow him to aid those who would listen and allow him to teach.

Ammaris stops and refocuses his attention. The battle ahead was going to be... difficult, a Dragon was virtually un-killable, even with sorcery, add chaos... He didn't finish the thought.

Ammaris sits on boulder and ponders, the key would be to destroy the chaos that pervades the Dragon. His theory was that without chaos the Dragon would die as it should have centuries before. The sorcerer nods to himself, he seemed to be doing that a lot, and standing sets off to face the Dragon.

*

Byrad had ordered his men to stand at the edge of the cliffs and wait for his signal. They only had about three quarters of an hour left before the spell wore off.

Byrad waits the time slipping by, then he sees Ammaris the sorcerer looks small and weak dressed in simple robes of dark green. Byrad sees one of the men shift and aim, quickly he moves to his side,

"Wait!" He hisses then looks down as the Dragon sees Ammaris.

The Dragon rears up and with a snarl opens its maw breathing flames at the sorcerer. When the inferno clears Byrad sees Ammaris stood in the centre of blackened heat split rock, unharmed. The Dragon roars again and then Byrad sees Ammaris' signal, he orders the men to fire and soon the creature is peppered with arrows.

The creature turns its decaying head and opens its maw, but before the flames can be let forth the Dragon shudders in pain, the head swings down and sees the sorcerer casting another spell. The Dragon ignores the arrows that were an annoyance only, focusing on the sorcerer that pains it. The Dragon leaps forward to crush the pitiful creature but it slams into an invisible wall. Then it feels the humans spell hit it and waits, there was no pain just a strange feeling of loss accompanied by tiredness.

Then the chaos side of the Dragon surges and it was clear what was happening. The sorcerer was removing chaos, destroying that which had kept it alive for so long. The Dragon feels chaos trying to control its mind, but now the Dragon understood. It was going to fight for release.

The Dragons wings flap and it lifts slightly, but the huge claws of its legs rip into the rock and holds it in range of the sorcerer. In desperation the chaos within the Dragon opens its mouth and breaths. Flame splashes against the invisible wall and proves ineffective, the blaze stop and the wings cease to flap, the Dragon settles back onto the mountain. Ammaris gasps and falls to his knees in exhaustion.

Byrad sees Ammaris' hand lift and he orders a cease fire.

The Dragons head drops to the ground near the sorcerer, a low rumbling voice echoes incoherently around the cliffs and Ammaris lays a hand on the Dragons head.

Slowly the Dragon turns to dust.

*

Byrad and the Eighty-eight find Ammaris still on his knees next to the Dragon dust.

"Ammaris?" Says Byrad.

The sorcerer looks up and smiles, "I'm fine Byrad."

"What happened?" Asks Byrad as he helps his friend to his feet.

"I removed chaos from the Dragon, which was all that kept it living. The arrows weakened the chaos enough for me to win, and the Dragon helped."

Byrad nods, "It was like the Dragon was fighting itself."

"It was." Says Ammaris as they head for the tomb, then he freezes, "Byrad draw your sword."

Instantly the Eighty-eight draw arrows to their bows and scan the area, Byrad unsheathes his sword. It was just plain iron, the friends let out a breath of relief.

"As I was saying, the Dragon fought to die, it had been infected by chaos since Dynadryds' time. That was why it attacked the town all those years ago." Ammaris stops at the doors. "It wanted to die."

The group enter the tomb and by Ammaris' light they see a hundred swords led on a hundred different stone coffins. The men look at Byrad but Ammaris answers their unspoken question.

"Take a sword, they are yours now. *You* are each a part of the Hundred. As in Dynadryds' time you will have swords of sorcery and be the vanguard of the army." With a slight pause and a hidden smile he adds, "Have faith in yourselves and what you wield. Byrad will lead as Warmonger, as did Dynadryd."

The men reverently take a sword and turn back to Byrad and chant his name, then following the lead of one soldier they kneel with swords before them and bow to Ammaris.

*

The new Hundred ride out of the tomb and head back through the mountains, behind them a wind picks up and the Dragon dust is lifted and blown away. Three eggs lie still upon the rock then small cracks appear on the shells.

Chapter Nineteen

The Eighty-eight with Byrad leading ride back to the town, they were wary and moved slowly with weapons in hand and horses at a slow trot. The soldiers had found that while the swords were in good condition, as sharp as when they were first forged and made into rune-swords, the leather hilt bindings had rotted away long ago thus each soldier bound his hilt to fit his hand.

Ammaris had studied the weapons and revealed the similarity to Byrads sword, each blade bore the enchanted sharpness and the warning glow. The sorcerer was awed at the amount of sorcery power expended into the blades, far more power than he had, even with his recent renewal.

As they edge closer to the town the Eighty-eight begin to relax, no more of Tammaras beings were waiting in ambush. In fact they had seen little of any creatures natural or otherwise, no Orcs, Trolls or any others that call Nogard Fell home. As they reach their first camp site they stop and prepare another. The soldiers are given instruction on the power of the swords and in the safest way to wield them, as Torran, Arnic and Kirin watch the men Byrad comes up to them and presents them with three of the swords.

"We lost some good men, but I think you deserve these swords." He holds them out and the three men take them, noting the new grips binding the hilts. They strap the swords to their backs beside the ones enchanted by Ammaris. Byrad looks over at the men, who had stopped their practice, Torran, Arnic and Kirin stride over to them shouting for them to resume.

*

Ammaris awakens to commotion and he quickly grabs his staff and leaves his tent. A group of soldiers drag one of Tammaras warriors into the camp.

It was a dark thing, big and powerful and black, man shaped but that was all the humanity left to it the rest was made from the essence that Tammara held.

As Ammaris comes to Byrads side he looks down on the creature and frowns, the mighty beast of chaos was asleep.

"How did you capture this?"

The men look at the sorcerer and shrug, "We found it outside a cave, Sir, and it was as if it were trying to reach it then collapsed into a deep sleep. It hasn't moved once since we began to drag it here, Sir."

Ammaris glances at Byrad then steps forward slowly. The sorcerer leans down and jumps back along with the rest of the men as the creature twitches an arm.

With pounding hearts the men stand with swords and magic at the ready, but the creature lays still again. Ammaris looks at the man who had reported, the soldier glances at the creature and back at the sorcerer.

"It never did that, Sir." He says with a defensive tone. The men relax slightly and a communal air of embarrassment seems to cover the group as they look on the quietly sleeping creature. Ammaris straightens his robes and clears his throat. Regaining his composure he studies the creature his gaze lingers on a point just in front of himself and not quite on the creature, he glances up and over his right shoulder then back down again.

"Be ready." He says then moves slowly forward.

As the sorcerer closes on the prostrate form of a Chaos-Warrior the men hold their breath and their gleaming swords. As Ammaris edges closer they all jump again as the creatures leg moves. Ammaris stops and watches, no other part of the creature moves and when he backs off the thing slips back into a restful sleep.

Letting out a breath of air, Ammaris turns to Byrad and grins, "Don't worry, it's harmless at present."

Byrad glances at the creature and back at his friend, "What is it?"

His grin broadening Ammaris replies, "It's *nocturnal*."

Byrad frowns a moment then a smile spreads across his face, "And when your shadow touched it..."

"...it awoke. If only that part that was in shadow." Finishes Ammaris with a grin.

Byrad and the sorcerer both stare down at the creature, the men wait patiently until they begin to glance at the deepening gloom. Arnic and Kirin glance at each other then step to Byrads side.

"Byrad," says Kirin "it is getting late."

Byrad looks at the sky and turns back to Ammaris, who still looks down on the creature stroking his goatee, "Ammaris what do we do now?" Asks the Lord of Branight.

Ammaris turns to his friend and purses his lips, "Take the men and wait over behind that ridge." The sorcerer indicates a rocky out cropping about two hundred meters away.

Byrad frowns, and is about to say something when Ammaris shakes his head, "Do not ask Byrad." Byrad hesitates a moment longer and then nods, turning to the men he orders them to retreat to the ridge and make camp.

Byrad waits at the ridge line, something makes him stay there and not even glance in the direction of his friend. Something in the way Ammaris had asked him to wait at the ridge, and also something in the agonized inhuman screams that echo around them from that direction. The screams had been going on for some time but Byrad could not say exactly how long.

He looks over at the men, they were deep in training with Arnic, Kirin and Torran practicing with the swords they would use against chaos. Byrad looks down at the tome of Élan-Vital, it seemed each of them had found an occupying activity to hide from the truth of what was happening.

Byrad looks up again and the men stop their training as the screams take on a frantic edge, then cease altogether. Turning Byrad looks over the ridge and watches as Ammaris makes his way to them, his feet drag as if in exhaustion and he leans on his pine-wood staff.

The sorcerer walks past Byrad and the men of the new Hundred. They all stare at Ammaris' face, it is white and his eyes were wide with horror and Byrad notices something else: Fear.

The sorcerer walks to his tent and disappears inside, before he goes he glances once at Byrad and the Lord hurries over.

As he enters the tent his eyes fall on the form of Ammaris sat on his bed, shivering as if with a chill.

Before Byrad can speak Ammaris begins, "Tammara is looking for the remnants of chaos." He states, "She plans to *be* the Chaos God."

Byrads mind spins as he tries to contemplate what he had heard, "How?"

Ammaris hugs himself within his robes and shakes, "Somehow before we met her, Tammara was infected with the essence of Chaos, which was a third of Chaos of old."

"What do you mean a third?" Interrupts Byrad.

Ammaris stands and begins to check his satchel, "Chaos of old was the being that was the head of the army against Dynadryd and the Four Kingdoms. When Karmarthen fought and destroyed Chaos it was separated into three parts: Mind, Body and Soul."

The sorcerer picks ups his staff and looks at Byrad, "Tammara has the Soul and looks for the Body. If she gains that and the Mind of Chaos then she will become the god that our ancestors defeated a millennia ago. Not just the half-god your God revealed her to be at this time." Ammaris frowns quietly adding, "Though she is probably better thought of as a third-god."

Byrad stares at his friend and nods his head, "So Tammara will become the god of chaos."

Ammaris shakes his head, "No. She will no longer be Tammara she will *be* Chaos. There will not be anything left of Tammara only Chaos will live."

Byrad looks down and rubs at his chin.

"Sinav Torlax Orinsu~ Hurth, Selniata"

Byrad looks up in sudden alarm as he hears the words, different but similar. He sees Ammaris disappear before his eyes a silver circle shimmering on the ground.

Byrad steps back from the circle and lowers his head, "Damn you Ammaris." He mutters then turns and exits the tent, "Break camp and form up!"

At Byrads command the eighty-eight are soon mounted and head back to Angar.

As the men reach the gates of the fortress town, two days later, they see a mass of frantic activity and when the guards see that they return a call is sent out for Gallant.

Byrad dismounts and walks towards Gallants palace, the lord of Angar is hurrying down the steps dressed in his armour. His face is drawn and weary looking and it is obvious he is relieved to see Byrad.

"Byrad!" Shouts Gallant over the noise of the town, it seemed as if every one was out on the streets and suddenly Byrad sees what they were doing: Packing.

"Gallant what's happening?" Byrad shouts over the noise, but before Gallant responds he drags him into a house stripped of the essentials and left empty by those who had once called it home.

With the door shut the noise seemed only loud rather than deafening, "What is happening?" Byrad repeats in a less of a shout.

Gallant rests against the table in the centre of the room and removes his silver gilded helm. Wiping the sweat from his brow with the back of a leather gauntlet he looks at Byrad directly, making eye contact as he speaks.

"The Border-Wall has fallen."

Byrad stares at Gallant a moment and then out of the window, the people were still rushing about, some were carrying food others were carrying clothing and blankets. Across the street Byrad could see a family sorting through their things, discarding that which was useless or unimportant for refugees. Byrad turns back to Gallant.

"What news of the armies?"

"Tammaras army is moving eastwards, our remaining forces are trying to slow them enough so the people from the cities of Erandor can make it here."

Byrad looks at Gallant and asks, "How far away are they?"

"The lead refugees are here now, but they stretch back for about a mile. I am just about to send three troops to guard them."

Byrad shakes his head, "No. The Hundred and I shall do that. Though I will need nine men to join with us for we lost that number and some in the mountains."

Gallants eyes widen, "You mean you did it. You got the swords?"

Byrad nods, "Yes. Are there men to fill the ranks?"

Gallant nods, "You may have the pick of the men here, but I ask for a place myself. Let me at least help *my* people."

Byrad notices the slight emphasis Gallant places on the word, but Gallant himself seems unaware of it. As they leave the relative quiet of the empty house and re-enter the noise of the town two of Gallants aides rush over.

"Your majesty," they say bending a knee, but quickly return to their feet, "The scouts report that the refugees are all in the vicinity, but Chaos-Beings are following."

Gallant nods and orders them to mobilise the twelve remaining troops, still at the north gate ready for any such occurrence.

As the two aides run off at full sprint Byrad asks, "Majesty?"

Gallant reddens in embarrassment as he dons his helm again, "Um, yes it seems I am now the King. With the prince and his father dead on the 'Wall I am the next in line, for the prince had not born a son and I was the Kings nephew."

Byrad recovers from his shock quickly and bends his knee, "Your majesty I am at your command."

Gallant raises Byrad to his feet and shakes his heads, "Thank you Byrad, but I have named you Warmonger of Erandor, you and I are equal during war."

Byrad has no time to accept his new standing, he waves to Arnic and they hurry to the north gate. When they reach the gate the three troops are already mounted and armed with cavalry sword and shield. They would join with the Hundred anyway, Byrad turns to Gallant and soon the King orders lances brought for the men.

The King mounts his own horse and the three hundred men strain to hear his words, "We are going to face the beings that have destroyed my uncle, your late King. The beings that destroyed the Crown Prince and any chance of his having a son to continue after him. I am your king now and we must save our people. We have very little to fight with, save our courage, our anger and our fear but we will fight to save the refugees.

Only the swiftest of Tammaras minions are close, these we must destroy. Will you ride with me and the Warmonger Byrad Branight?"

A resounding roar of acceptance blasts forth from three hundred throats and it would have continued had Gallant not raised his hands, "The Warmonger asks that eight volunteers come forward to wield the mystical blades of the Hundred, but listen to him first."

Byrad looks at the men before him they were aching to volunteer, all three hundred but as he stares at them he sees that some have seen the weapons, Byrad lifts one of the swords and shows it to the men.

"I need those who are the best with this type of blade, as you see it is a stabbing and slashing weapon but it is made of iron not steel. It is heavy to use in combat, more cumbersome than the swords you have used in the past."

As Byrad looks at the men now, he sees that most have realised their lack of ability with such a weapon but some still have a look Byrad can understand, "These weapons are a great and powerful magic, but they remain a *weapon* they will not guard you from harm. It is your own ability that will accomplish that and your own ability that will strike down the Chaos-Beings."

Now only a fraction of the men look ready to volunteer and under Byrads gaze those few who know their comrades to be the best force them to step forward. Byrad hands them each a blade and they take their place with the Hundred.

With that the small army, made up of The Hundred and some two hundred and ninety-two cavalry armed with lances head to the north and form a rearguard at the back of the refugee column and wait. In the distance they can see scouts ranging back and forth, then they head for the town.

The first to spot the King quickly gives his report.

"There are some five hundred Chaos-Beings moving fast this way, they will reach us in about twenty minutes."

The line forms up and Gallant sends the scouts to the city with orders to evacuate all non military to the plains. Then they wait for the chaos to begin.

The Line waits as the refugees escape to the town, and beyond into the plains of the nomads. They wait as the fastest of the Chaos-Beings race towards them.

As the scout had said some five hundred Chaos-Beings approach, but as those beings see The Line they slow and the great Chaotic mass of Tammaras minions amble forward intent and deadly.

A stillness settles over the opposing forces and the men of The Line grip their lances grimly, the Mass trample forward.

177

Byrad slowly draws his sword and The Hundred follow his lead, the glow of a hundred and one enchanted blades almost defeats the sunlight, and the Chaos-Beings pause and stare at the sorcery held before them.

With a sudden shout that breaks the silence Byrad leads the charge into the Mass, the shout is taken up by all, even those who have never been to the place.

"BRANIGHT!" the word blasts from The Line as they surge forward into the Mass.

The horsemen charge and the lances pierce the Chaos-Beings, leaving them to be trampled by horse and their own alike. With few unhorsed they ride on and turn for a second charge, the Chaos-Beings fight with a frenzy but the Hundred slay them where they stand, and they herd them about so the horsemen can attack again.

The Line slowly decimates the Mass but still the Chaos-Beings fight, men of The Line fall and are ripped apart but others take up the fallen lance when their own break, or they take up the fallen blades of the Hundred and return to the fight. As the sun sets the Line closes down on the Mass which have lost most of their number, with almost inhuman determination the Line moves forward slaying as they go. Chaos-Beings fall under the assault of enchanted blades and heavy lance, until finally the last of the Mass are crushed.

Silences and stillness return to The Line as the fading sunlight attempts to retake its glory that was stolen by the swords of the Hundred. Those swords give up their glow as the last of the Mass die. All about the road to Angar the bodies of the Mass lie still, shattered lances and fallen men join them in death as equals. The men of The Line dismount and lift their dead comrades to horseback, turning away from the north ignoring the approaching Host that heads towards them. With silent dignity The Line returns to the town and follows the refugees to the plains.

The dawn breaks bright and sunny above the plains, the refugees and the army move steadily south. They had stopped long enough at the trading station to evacuate it then they pressed on into the night. Such was the intensity of the refugees that the traders never argued but simply nodded, packed up and joined the migration south.

Byrad rides before the Hundred and those of The Line that had survived, about hundred and fifty. They ride behind their lord at a discreet distance still bloodied with bandages soaked in blood, new lances held upright. Every so often one of The Line turn to look north, looking for the Host that chases them, what they see is the fallen mountains that block the pass to Angar.

The Pass had always been the last form of defence for the town, it had been developed to block the pass and stop any advancement by an enemy from the south, now it had been used in the reverse and blocked the advance of Tammaras army. The defence mechanism was such that a carefully rigged avalanche could be started, it would collapse the mountain and fill the pass with stone creating an impassable barrier for the enemy. Now the enemy was trapped in the pass and the refugees headed south in relative safety.

Another rider turns and looks, for though they had stopped the advance of the Host the refugees were not fool enough to believe that they were entirely safe. It would take time but the Chaos-Beings would get through the pass and fall upon them in furious destruction.

Byrad turns slightly and looks to the north then he turns back to his conversation with a woman riding beside him. He had not seen her since his first night in Angar, but he had met her again after his return from the battle. They had spent much time together and as soon as they reached the City of Hope he would make her his wife.

Suddenly a rider cries out in alarm, Byrad turns and sees him pointing to the north a small group of Chaos-Beings had scaled the blocked pass and rushed after them. They were distant but gaining at an amazing rate.

With a curse Byrad turns his horse and the Hundred and the men of The Line race to the rear of the refugees and prepare for a battle, while still following. They would wait until they *had to* fight.

Over the next four hours the refugees hurry south as fast as they could, the Chaos-Beings were still at a distance but soon they would be too close.

Byrad glances at his men, some he did not know others he did, like Arnic and Kirin, Gallant and Zanric, Torran. But even if he did not know the men he did trust them, they had fought the Chaos-Beings together and they were well aware of the power of those Beings. Taking a look back down the line of refugees Byrad spots his wife to be, and then orders his men to turn and face the approaching Chaos-Beings. Byrad utters a quiet prayer to Élan-Vital and draws his sword, his men follow suit and form The Line once more.

*

The Life God sits up straight as he hears a faint prayer from Byrad, with the sudden insight he gains the god calls the others and soon the twelve gods appear.
"What is it brother?" Asks Ackza as he steps from his shadowy home.
"Byrad returns from the north and he brings the hosts of Tammara following behind. We must help him reach the City."
The others look at each other and War shifts his armoured form.
"What can we do? We can not fight Tammaras creations." The voice of the powerful god almost shakes with his helplessness.
Ackza sneers at him, "There are many ways to fight. You should know that, War."
War turns his helmeted head to look at the twin but says nothing, Élan Vital steps forward and the gods look to him.
"We may not be able to destroy chaos but we can slow them down, give Byrad a chance to reach the city and make a stand against Tammara."
The other gods quickly grasp the idea and begin to use their power to aid their only perceived hope. The gods each use their own area of power and the plains before The Line is soon a maelstrom of divine power.
Laumas-Nahtan, Earth God shakes the very foundations of the plains creating gaping chasms that steam with heat from the molten core of the world.
Immoha, Sun God blasts the plains with the power of the sun, sapping the very moisture from the air its self.
Zumithia, Night Goddess steals the light from the sky, turning the baking plains black as the darkest night.

Corinthia, Moon Goddess casts her light in a confusing pattern over the plains, leading the chaos beings into chasms and turning them away from their intended route.

Trickster lays a hand across the line and gives them the sight to see through the darkness.

War, Battle God summons forth his berserk rage and drops it into the minds of those who would accept it, and the Erandish were of a berserk nature when it came to the Chaos-beings.

Hakim, Hunting God calls forth the beasts of the plains, and soon lions, panthers and Wyrms join the humans.

Insitina, Agricultural Goddess draws forth the plants of the plains and forces them to grow, creating a dense forest of grasses.

Tempest, Storm God creates his storms, thunder crashes and lightening spears into the ground. The rain and hail lash down like arrows from a million bows.

The twins grant their aid as well. Ackza, Underworld God commands his legions of wraiths, ghosts and other undead to join The Line, and his brother Élan Vital, Life God protects the men from wounds.

*

Byrad and the Line stare first at the sudden maelstrom before them, and then at the strange multitude of creatures that fill their ranks. As the Chaos-Beings leave the maelstrom these allies attack them without hesitation.

Byrad belatedly gives the word and The Line surges forward, some of the men suddenly scream and go into a berserk rage. Those with enchanted swords lay about themselves oblivious to the wounds they receive, and the murderous fury destroys the momentum of the Chaos-Beings. The men on horse back charge in on the 'Beings and those who loose their mounts drag free their own normal, mundane weapons and even manage to hack and slash the Chaos-Beings into death.

Byrad slams his shield into the 'face' of one 'Being and with a back hand slash decapitates another. with a shout he calls a retreat and The Line moves back, as the Chaos-Beings pick themselves up and advance the maelstrom descends on them and obliterates them from view. Screams of rage and of pain reach The Line, but

Byrad turns his men about and they race after the fleeing refugees.

As they come in behind the last of them, Byrad orders his men to report their condition. The men of The Line report somewhat in awe that there are few casualty's and only four deaths and they were seen to have been ripped apart during the battle. But those same men were also seen to destroy many of the enemy, with only their broken lances and their broadswords.

"How did they do that?" Murmurs Arnic.

"It would seem," Byrad says, "Tammaras forces are not as invulnerable as we thought. Brute force seems to have as much effect on them as sorcery."

*

Even with the maelstrom protecting the rear of the fleeing refugees, and Byrads forces, the continuing two week march was difficult. The strain of hard travel was a problem for the Erandish people, but they marched on with little complaint. They knew that sore feet and aching legs were a far better discomfort than the Chaos-Beings would meet out.

During the march south Byrad and Gallant both noticed a slight disturbance in the refugees. At camp one night a large majority of the people approach the two men, the delegated spokesman bowed to his King and the Warmonger.

"Majesty, Lord Byrad. We are troubled, when will we take back our homes?"

Gallant looks at the man before him and nods in understanding, "When Tammara is defeated we will return to Erandor and take back our homes."

The people nod but the man asks another question, "To that end we volunteer for the army. Some of us have been in service before and the others are willing to train."

Gallant and Byrad look at the people before them, seeing the determination on the faces of the men and women.

Gallant turns to Byrad and whispers, "It is your choice they will be under your command."

Byrad nods and stands, "Your King has given me command of all the Erandish forces. You will come to me tomorrow evening and you shall join the army. You will be trained night and day and by the end of our

182

two week journey I will expect you to be an army trained and disciplined."

In surprising chorus the new army salute the Warmonger and the King with resounding shout of *"Yes Sir!"*

The training of the new army was overseen by both Byrad and Gallant. The King gives his experience he had developed in training the recruits at Angar, and Byrad shows the men and women how to fight. The day saw the new army being given fitness training, they were forced to run a circling route around the refugees that were not part of the army, and given the determination of the people they were gaining in stamina and strength. Two requirements for surviving the Chaos Host.

During the night the army were trained in the use of weapons, and due to their recent findings the weapons were the heaviest and most damaging they had. The arms merchants that had joined the refugees at the trading station were commissioned to supply those weapons. There were the pole axe and halberd, the maul and great hammers, great axes and great swords.

The training focussed the defences on dodging and parrying, and on the development of companion defence (the art of defending the person beside you, as the troops would not have the use of shield).

As the training progressed along with the travel through the plains, the native tribes of the nomads joined them. Most were of the newly converted to Byrads religion, but they were all escaping the maelstrom and the roaming Chaos Beings.

Just before the group reached the edge of the plains, and the north road to Branight the Erandish come before Byrad and their King.

"What can we do for you?" Asks Gallant to the spokesman, the same as the one who had come asking to become soldiers.

"Your majesty, we are aware of the secret Lord Byrad has kept from us." States the man.

Gallant nods, "I see." He turns to Byrad and motions for him to step forward.

The Warmonger stands before the people and looks out at them, waiting.

"What secret have you discovered?"

The spokesman looks at Byrad and speaks, "My Lord you are a religious man, you are the head priest of a

God." The words are spoken without accusation, just simple fact.

Byrad nods, "Yes I am the High priest of Élan-Vital. He is my God and he is God of Life, with his aid..." Byrad stops as he sees the spokes man lift his hand in a stopping motion.

"We are not concerned with your god, we are concerned with you. Will you do all you can against Tammara, she is a god also."

Byrad is stunned, "Yes of course..."

"Good" interrupts the man, "We will follow you still and I will say only this, do not speak of your god to us Erandish, we are not interested, your choice is to worship a god, ours is to not." The man bows and turns with the rest to continue with their training. Tomorrow they would reach the City and they all wanted to be ready to take their place with the defenders.

The sight of the city was a spur to the weary troops and to Byrad it was a home coming. He looks at the city and notices a flag, from this distance he could not make out whose it was but it was customary to show the flag of visiting noblemen in Branight.

Slowly Byrad leads the people to Branights' gates and into the Four-kingdoms. Byrad rides in and looks upon the new fortifications he had had started before he went north. Now the walls were thicker and atop them four massive catapults, their crews stand watching the north waiting for the army of Chaos. Byrad was impressed by the fact that the men's attention was focussed and did not waver to curiosity at the disciplined troops of refugees, men and women, with their children and old folk beside them.

Byrads gaze lifts as he passes through the gate and he now sees the flag is of the Grovian King, his cousin Caervil Cron. As he looks back he sees his cousin walking towards him along with a great many priests of Élan-Vital.

"Caervil," says Byrad as he dismounts and greets the King, "It's good to see you."

Caervil Cron was a short man, quick of movement with shoulder length black hair. He walks quietly and much about him gives credence to the rumours that the King of Grovia was once a thief, trained and accomplished.

Of course that was many years ago before he became King, still Byrad had an idea that his cousin still continued with his nocturnal activities.

"Byrad it is good to see you, your priests were worried."

Byrad nods and shakes his cousins hand, who looks into his eyes, "You are weary, go to your rooms we shall deal with the host you bring." He looks over the thousands of troops marching in through the city gates.

With sudden weariness Byrad nods. As Caervil and the officers begin to billet the new troops and the refugees, Byrad is led away by some priests, while others move to the troops to offer healing. These receive cold stares leaving the priests to stand in puzzlement, as Herbalists and Physicians from the refugees begin checking on their patients.

Chapter Twenty

The following days were filled with the preparations of the defences, and the integration of the Erandish troops into the infantry and cavalry. The infantry and cavalry were issued with the new armour and with the best weapons available. Work had begun on creating lances with the new alloy, but they would not be ready for at least four weeks. Four weeks that they probably didn't have.

Every day brought more troops to the city. The Kingdom of Gorst had sent its army led by the priests of War and their own King, and reports from the returning messengers were that the Kingdoms of Sala and Mercia were sending their own armies. Even the City Provinces of Eastwater, Deep-port, and Trading were sending parts of their own City militia. The stories of the Horde that faced the City of Hope had spread across the lands like wildfire, all who heard of the proposed defence at Branight came to help in any way possible. Not only with arms and the will to fight but also with harvests and the baking of breads, smiths came to give their services in the forging of iron, bowyers lent their aid and the young and old prepared for the inevitable casualties.

The priests also saw to their duties each of the religions set up holy sanctuaries to their gods for use by those that would seek solace and healing. The religions were under strict rules by order of the Warmonger to cease any and all hostilities between each other.

On the first day of the second week of being back at his city, Byrad sits in the council throne room that had become the war room. The newly arrived kings of Gorst, Sala and Mercia were sat around a table shouting. They had been arguing for the last three hours about Byrads status as Warmonger.

"I will not relinquish my command to a boy!" Roars the King of Gorst, a huge man powerfully muscled with a massive grey streaked beard and almost fanatical ideas about war, as all Kings of Gorst were.

He as the twelfth to be crowned was proud of his heritage. "If any here should be sole commander it should be I."

Byrad opens his mouth to reply when the King of Sala shakes his head, "Gorst, you will not command my troops, they would return to their families, your legacy of tactics would have them all dead!"

Gorst stares at the King of Sala, a tall thin man dressed in silks, clean shaven and pale haired, "To die in war is an honour. We should strive to have the most valiant death and be remembered in legend."

As the two kings continue to argue Byrads anger rises until he stands and draws his sword, slamming it down onto the table. The Kings stop in mid shout and turn to look at the Lord of Branight.

"I lay my sword on the table of war, I ask that you lay your swords with mine, this is my city and what we face will affect us all. If we do not unite under one leader it will be the death of all our people." Byrad turns to Gorst and stares at him, "I may be a boy in your eyes but I am lord here, if you do not defer to me you can take your men and return to your own land and wait for Tammara to come to you." He looks at the King of Sala, "The same is said to you. I will have command of your men or you can have command in your peoples last hours. Decide now."

The two Kings stare at Byrad for long moments, tension strong in the air. Then the King of Mercia, quiet throughout the three hours of debate stands and draws his broad sword, laying it down on the table, "You have my men, you are Warmonger of the Mercian army."

The King of Sala purses his lips then nods, he draws his scimitar and places it on the table, "You have my army as well."

Byrad looks at the King of Gorst and waits. The King frowns then a slight smile plays across his bearded lips, which split into a grin as he draws his sword, a huge two handed thing, "Very well boy, you will be Warmonger and we shall follow your lead." He lays his sword on the table also and Byrad thanks them, and they begin to discuss the best tactics for the impending battle.

As the days end and begin anew and the maelstrom continues to hold, the forces at Branight continue to grow as more men come to their call. The twin Lord Rulers of Deep-Port and Eastwater arrive and soon pledge their men to Byrad, as does the Commander of the Trading Militia. Finally there are but a few hundred men and women arriving from all parts of the Four Kingdoms, seeking a place in the biggest army any can remember. Gallant and Caervil train the new recruits and soon they are deemed ready to stand with the rest of their people, to hold back the Hordes of Chaos.

Byrad sits at the war table with all those in command at the city.

"What is the final number of men?" Asks Byrad

Gallant looks down at some notes and after a moment answers, "With the last group of volunteers, we have an army of one-hundred an ninety-two thousand, plus the twenty-five thousand Erandish, which includes the one-hundred and fifty Cavalry of the Line with your hundred, a total of two-hundred and seventeen thousand one hundred."

Gorst laughs and smacks the table, "Those chaos things will never survive an army that size."

Gallant looks up at the man and smiles grimly, "The army that was put against them in my country was close to five-hundred thousand. We have just one thousand men left from that army, and many of them are still wounded."

Gorst chokes on his laughter at Gallants calm words and sits back as Byrad nods at the figure given.

"The walls of Branight need a total of six thousand men, with the rest in reserve we have a chance of holding."

Torran stares out of a window, a mug of ale in hand, "For how long?" he asks without looking round.

Byrad looks grim as he answers, "For as long as possible, we must give Ammaris the time to stop Tammara."

The others look doubly grim, they had been told of Ammaris and his sorcery. Some were wary of trusting to him, of trusting a Sorcerer, and the others who had met him were aware of the scarcity of his success, even for a Sorcerer.

After a moment of silence Byrad stands, "Get some rest, and we shall meet again in the morning."

Torran drains his mug and muttering leaves first. Byrad hearing his lieutenants words had to agree, they would meet again as long as Tammara stayed away and the Maelstrom lasted.

Walking to the altar Byrad kneels and prays to his God, as he did every day and night waiting for the word that meant Ammaris had failed, that Tammara had returned.

Finally the word came, forty-six days since Ammaris had abruptly left, Byrad receives a warning from his god.

Byrads first thought was for Ammaris, he had failed to stop Tammara from regaining the physical form of chaos and that could mean only one thing.

Byrad brushes the thought away and quickly gathers the commanders and tells them of his gods message.

"How long do we have?" Asks Gallant, but as alarm bells ring on the north wall the King of Erandor has his answer.

Quickly they race for their commands, Byrad gathers his Hundred and hurries to the walls above the gates. As he reaches his position he sees the Maelstrom was down, that meant Tammara was leading her army through the northern hills of Branights border. The defenders wait for the first of the horde to appear.

The City of Hope was deathly quiet as those on, and behind the walls wait for the Horde. For a seeming ageless time nothing appears and it seems the entire world holds its breath. The defenders shift uneasily and Byrad draws his sword, the Sword of Branight.

It glows brightly and as all the men ready their weapons a hundred glows dot the north wall. To the west the horizon darkens as the sun sets.

Then in the twilight gloom the Horde come screaming through the hills into Branights borders. They are led by Tammara seeming unchanged, with her blonde hair and small form out of place with the mass of warped and twisted forms around her.

She leads them to the shores of the Lake of Night and the shattered bridge. She turns as the defenders on the walls watch straining to see how they would cross, for the waters were fast and deep and most would not chance crossing it.

Tammara points to the water and the biggest of her warriors lurch forward, wading into the deadly flow. Soon a massive, living bridge crosses from one side to the other and the Horde come onwards.

As they watch the Horde the catapult crews prepare their machines, and over the next few moments boulders crash down. Even though a great many of the Chaos-warriors were crushed the others simply ran over the rocks or around them, trampling the wounded and dead.

Again and again the boulders were released to slam into the Horde, but still they come onwards and then, far too quickly, they were too close for the catapults to be of any use.

Byrad lifts his sword to the sky and the men prepare themselves, the priests of the many different Gods come forward upon the wall and all the defenders wait. The Chaos-warriors scrabble forward, as they reach the city some hammer the walls and gates while others leap onto them and scale them with clawed hands.

Byrad gives a shout and burning oil is tipped down upon the Chaos-warriors. Soon creams of pain and the stench of burnt things cover the walls, but still they climb on burnt and blistered.

Another command from Byrad and the hundreds of priests lift their arms in prayer, and as each of the Gods answer, the world around Branight changes.

First the darkened sky is lit as the sun rises again, all across the Horde Chaos-warriors fall into their nocturnal slumbering, those that were on the walls simply loose their grip and crash onto their brethren.

Then, from a cloudless sky thunder rumbles and lightning slashes across the Horde ripping more from the walls. Next the plants and roots beneath the feet of the Horde rise up and they are dragged down and crushed. Then the very earth itself rises up and seems to swallow some of the Horde. Next a shadow falls over the Horde and those of the weakest minds turn and flee from the City. Then some among the Horde seem to blur and their features shift and a quarter of them look like those they attempt to fight. Those that are left turn on these 'men' and attack them only to find the illusions fade as they rip their own apart.

Over the next 'day' the Horde and Tammara are in disarray as the priests continue to call on their gods, until finally the priests begin to fall as they give themselves to their deities. As each priest falls the miracles cease and Tammara draws her forces together again.

Byrad orders the priests, those that remain to halt their efforts and soon the sky is dark and the thunder stops, the world returning to the natural.

Tammara's forces rise up as those who were slumbering in the false day awaken, and those that were forced to flee in fear returned. Again Tammara sends the forces at the city and this time blood would flow from the defenders.

As the first of the Horde reach the top of the wall the defenders attack them, pushing them back before they can take a stand on the battlements. Soon as the Horde push upwards the defenders are forced backwards and true battle begins. Byrad and The Hundred hack at the Chaos-warriors and they die, though some of the defenders also die. Those beside the fallen pick up the swords of the hundred and attack the attackers again.

Those defenders that were of Branight fought with out the aid of the enchanted blades, but they used their hate, anger and the fact that they defended their home to give them the strength to hold.

The Erandish were of the same ilk, though they fought with the berserk rage that came from the loss of their home, and even the Chaos-warriors quailed at the ferocity of the men and women. As more and more fell on each side more moved from the ranks of reserves, and though a great many died in the Horde, many also perished in the ranks of the defenders. As Byrad and the commanders rallied the men there came up onto the wall priests of Ackza and those of Élan-Vital. They had held back from the first battle of the religions, but now they too lift their arms in prayer. All across the wall men who had wounds found them healed, those who were weary found their strength return, and those who were dead rose again, restored to life by the joined might of the two gods.

Quickly Byrad attacks anew and the restored men of the wall fight with the will of those with only one choice, be they the truly alive or those with but borrowed life. Slowly the forces of Hope close down the Chaos-warriors attack and push them back, whittling them down and destroying them until they were at the battlements again. From the field outside the walls Tammara screams in rage and her forces retreat to her side.

A ragged bloodied line of Defenders stare out at them, and though they had won none cheer for this was but the first battle. To the east the sun rises in true dawn and the forces of chaos thin as those nocturnal fall.

Tammara stares at Byrad and in the silence Byrad shivers.

During the day Tammara simply stands amid her Horde and stares at city. Byrad had long since turned away and though he busied himself with the details of burial, (the borrowed life had been taken back at the end of the battle) he could almost feel her gaze still. The Defenders were taking rest and food that the day had unexpectedly given them. As the burials were finished Byrad turns to the facts of the fighting.

In just one night they had lost some nine-thousand men and women, including about 40 or so priests of the various religions that had joined the fight.

Those priests left tend to the injured and though the Erandish were pure heathens, they saw the need and when offered aid they accepted.

As the hours wore by and the forces both wait the Defenders were soon all healed and asleep. Those that had not fought on the walls watching Tammara watching them.

The setting sun brings activity from both sides, the Chaos-warriors stand and race forward the Defenders set themselves for the next battle.

Again the smoke of burning oil and chaos flesh floats above the wall as the Defenders and the Chaos-warriors fight back and forth. They nearly over whelmed the defenders but with a furious onslaught the Chaos was forced back and the stale mate continued. With the dead men falling and rising and falling again, the defenders fought to the last man on the walls and beyond. The reserves push forward from both sides filling the gaps and continuing the fight.

Still the priests' move through the battle aiding those Defenders that need such aid.

At the close of that night the chaos was repelled again, but this time the toll was worse for the Defenders. As the last burial is completed the total that night was twelve-thousand.

The commanders meet with Byrad and over the course of the day, it is decide that at the morning next the battle would be taken to the enemy.

That night the battle was fought as hard as every other and the Defenders threw themselves at the chaos, men and women twisting away from claws and teeth, hacking and slashing, hammering and bludgeoning the Chaos-Warriors. The dead and living were ferocious in the battle and the Chaos-warriors were routed again and again, only to return with more and the battle would begin anew.

Finally the dawn arose and the fighters split apart again. As the last Chaos-warrior left the wall, the Defenders adjusted their armour and joined the rest of the army below behind the gates. Byrad turns to the men and women and without a word he bows to them turning as the doors are flung open as the sun lifts into the sky.

Tammara stands watching, and as the Defenders run out into The Horde a look of surprise flickers across her face, then she orders her armies up and the battle begins once again.

The Defenders have their cavalry now and the lances rip into them again and again, Zanric leads the charge picking away at the edges of The Horde. Those on foot crash into the enemy and the fighting that echoes around the valley of Branight is deafening in its noise.

The screams of the dying mingle with the battle cries of the living, the clanging of claw on armour and shield is muted by that of the sword, axe and hammer on bone and flesh.

For many long hours the fighting moves around the entrance of Branight, then as the two sides regroup a shout comes from the lips of the Defenders.

In the distance hundreds of shapes are seen flying in the blue sky. Byrad strains to see and he grows cold as he recognises the approaching doom, voices raise the shout in his mind: *Dragons*.

"To the city!" Screams Byrad and as one the Defenders flee the battlefield and race for the city. The Chaos-warriors scream, with murderous lust they chase after the fleeing men. Tammara slowly turns and looks at the Dragon flight, led by three Dragons there were at least a hundred of the black, bat winged monsters.

Byrad and rest race through the gates and they slam in the face of the Horde. The Defenders reach the wall and watch as the Dragons swoop down. Byrad closes his eyes and a groan slips from him as he sees the end of life, not only for the defenders but for the people of the Four Kingdoms too.

The Warmonger begins to pray when he hears a ripple of confusion from the men around him. Opening his eyes he stares first at Tammara as she stands watching the Dragons, then he looks to the Dragons and sees them turn away from the city, as he watches a cheer rises from the City of Hope.

The Dragons' breath splashes across the field that had seen battle, and engulfing the Chaos-warriors and their master. It strikes all beyond the city and nothing can be seen through the inferno.

The Defenders turn away from the heat and the flame, then it stops and the Dragons turn back to the north.

Tammara was no more.

Chapter Twenty-One

The City of Hope was silent as the men and women of The Defenders stare at the black mass of the Chaoswarriors. The war was finished.
The Defenders move off the wall and walk out of the incinerated gates, they stop as the heat grows too much and they look out over the devastation.
The Defenders sink to their knees and Byrad rips of his helm and laughs and cries as he looks at the end of Chaos.
Then, through his tears he sees movement. Dashing away the tears he stares at the place and sees it again, then from out of the black mass Tammara stands up.

She was so badly burnt that half her face was gone, leaving just black bone showing. Her body is in a worse state, burnt into a hunched and crooked form, a chaotic form of herself.
She stares at Byrad and stumbles forward, the Defenders stare in horror then she falls.
As she staggers to her feet again she screams, a horrible sound of anguish. As the men and women watch she rears back and her body breaks the set of her fire hardened skin. Then her body is seemingly ripped apart from within, and in her stead stands a thing of red skin and rippling muscles. As it stretches to its full height, some twelve feet or more, its head comes into view, a massive black skull like that of a ram, horns curling up at the side. It sees Byrad and with a single bound it is before him. The Defenders are stunned and unmoving as the creature roars into Byrads face.
Byrad lifts his blazing sword but the creature slams a fist into his chest launching him backwards. As the Defenders rouse, it slaughters them bodies flung to the walls to smash or into the black mass of the field where they burst into flame.

Byrad lies on the ground, pained and stunned he looks down and sees the curve of his breast plate is now

inverted. He looks away and sees Torran at his side a look of terror on his face.
Byrad follows his wide eyed gaze and sees Chaos destroy his people, then the thing that had been Tammara approaches. Byrad scrabbles for his sword but it is just beyond his reach, he shouts to Torran but the scout seems not to hear.

*

Arnic forces himself up, his broken body barely working he crawls forward and reaches for his discarded sword. The infusion of vitality aids a little and he looks to Kirin, he was also in a bad way. Arnic then looks to Byrad and he sees his Lord scrabbling for his sword and not reaching it. He sees Torran and he shouts to the scout much as Byrad and Kirin were doing.

*

Kirin shouts out at Torran. He could see Tammara approach the two men and Torran just stands there shaking, then Kirin's shout changes as does Arnic's. "NO!!"

*

Torran turns and flees Chaos, he races south through the city passing a fast moving horse and rider. Torran runs and not once looks back, his sword dims as he escapes his terror.

*

Byrad tries to back away from Chaos...

*

Ammaris gallops through the City of Hope, he passes Torran as he flees and then the sorcerer sees Tammara...

*

Byrad stares up at Chaos and it stares at him, then it slams its talons into his chest. The metal forged by the dwarven smiths in Dynadryd's time buckles but does not break. With a roar of rage the thing that had once been Tammara reaches down...

*

Ammaris sees Tammara in her new form, straddling Byrad its hands at the Warmongers head, at his friends head. The thing looks up at his approach and stares him in the eye.
Ammaris screams.

*

Byrad tries to get away from the hands of the creature, but as he hears a scream from Ammaris he looks up into the eyes of Tammara. His own scream is ended as she rips his head from his body.

Tammara lifts the dripping head and shows it to the world. Arnic and Kirin stagger at the sight and they fall, then with a wild cry the Defenders every last one, attacks her. The two guards scream incoherently and they join in the madness of the Defenders.

Arnic and Kirin hack and slash at her dragging free their second blades, enchanted by Ammaris, they attack in a fury. The Hundred join the melee as do the Kingdoms forces and the Erandish. Tammara roars with pain but she fights back and scatters the Defenders, leaving them broken on the streets of Branight.

She turns as a horse and rider come to a stop, and she sees Ammaris. With a roar she turns and leaps away, racing north faster than anything of nature could. As she leaves five huge Chaos-warriors crash through the north wall, they were all burnt and blackened, but living still.

Ammaris' eyes narrow but he had not the power to destroy them, not after his recent battle. He slips from his horse as they advance upon him, and his eyes glimpse a faint blue glow from Byrads body. Wondering the Sorcerer touches his staff to the body, he murmurs the command and the strength of power that flows to him forces him to his knees.

The creatures seem to sense what had happened, for as Byrads body turns to dust and Ammaris stands leaning on his staff they rush at him. With a laugh Ammaris attacks.

Epilogue

Ammaris stares at the remains of Byrad. Around him the dead Chaos-warriors lie still, the Defenders gather to him and they stand in silence.
Byrad was gone but his death had meant that they had all survived. Now was the task of finding a new leader, a new Warmonger so that when Tammara returned she would be destroyed in Byrads name.
The men and women lift the armour of Byrad and they walk to the Church, to the Palace of Branight and Byrads home.

The author

Neil James Hobbs was born in Swindon in April 1978. He was never much for books till he was 13 and saw the "Lord of the Rings" animation on a Sunday afternoon in the winter. The next day he went to school and asked for the book. It took him three months to read it and he was hooked on books ever since. (his brother can verify that as his books kept mysteriously disappearing)
He has an old friend, well house mate Emily, a french girl, who inspired him to actually think of getting the novel he was writing as a hobby published and after he met his good friend John who was also trying to write he finally managed to finish it. Now in 2007 he has finally published it.
Many more novels are planned.